Through A Wind

A *Skylark in the* **l**

Helyna L. Clove

Helyna L. Clove
♥

Copyright © 2024 by Helyna L. Clove
Written and edited by Helyna L. Clove
Published by Helyna L. Clove
Cover art by Harkalé Linaï - https://harkale.art
Cover design by Helyna L. Clove
Interior formatting and design by Helyna L. Clove
All rights reserved. No part of this publication may be reproduced, distributed or transmitted in any form or by any means, without prior written permission.
This is a work of fiction. Names, characters, places, and events are a product of the author's imagination. Any resemblance to actual people, living or dead, or to businesses, companies, events, institutions, or locales is completely coincidental.

Table of Contents

1 1
2 9
3 25
4 41
5 53
6 67
7 85
8 109
Acknowledgements 117
About the Author 119

For every scared, hopeful wanderer

1

The Candle was packed with people that night—just like every night of late.

Creatures of many origins and semblances sat, crouched, or slouched around low metal tables in the moody sunset-orange lighting of the room. Those alone wrapped themselves into silence, buried in their food and drinks, and those in company were generally being a nuisance, loudly debating news or future destinations with friends and colleagues, celebrating fortunate deals, or grieving losses of man or power. The planet Duplex, and this muddy town, Blackbones, had become a popular destination for all species newly freed from the tyrannical rule of the Union, but human or alien, there was never a lack of interesting faces in the Candle.

Noll Morgan glanced over the room, blinking slowly. The remains of her dinner—some kind of dish made of spicy fish—stared back at her from the plate. It was decent food but too oily for her taste. Jayce would have shoveled the scraps into his mouth in half a second, except her twin brother had gone out to do stars know what in the pouring rain an hour or so ago. He was probably getting thoroughly soaked and into some grade-A trouble right about now.

Good for him. But watching dark water splash against the plexiglass of the restaurant windows in waves with the intense gusts of wind, heavy gray rainclouds looming in the sky above, Noll decided she was satisfied with her choice. Keeping warm, out of the rain, and eating reasonably well—that was ideal. A flickering lightning strike peered into the building, immediately followed by the groan and gradually sharpening crackle of thunder. The storm was right above them. Or more precisely, above the Window.

Her glance shifted back to the room. Jayce could have stayed in if he wanted trouble—that, too, came with all the "interesting faces" on a relatively independent planet. Especially with the rules of the galaxy changing recently, following the whole ordeal with the Talalan lane manipulator apparently almost imploding space-time, the end of the decades-long Miyozan war, and the Union Leadership's sudden change of heart regarding the subjugation of all sentient beings. Noll had heard it all. Got fed up with it pretty quickly, too.

But that whole chaos had been why the lanehunter clans sent their scientists over here a few months ago to finally try and harness the opportunities provided by the Window—the strange gateway Duplex was known for. No one had bothered with this place for a long time—it was too troublesome—but Noll supposed the need to replace the hideouts her people had lost in their last clashes with the Union was motivation enough. Perhaps they thought they could do something tricky with it like on the Ranch, the lanehunter homeworld. Who knew? It was all the same to her, except upon hearing about the hubbub, Jayce wanted to make the trip from Metallia to see what was up. Noll was less enthused, but in the end, they'd come here on their trusty old ship, the *Taro*, a week ago.

As it turned out, lots of fucking rain—that's what was up. Or rather down, and around, and in between, and all over everything.

And even though no one knew what exactly everyone else was up to, the town swarmed with all kinds of people trying to find their path after the latest big upheaval. Lanehunters, Net spies, aliens, and even Union deserters flocked together, and although the bizarre congregation was a recipe for catastrophe in theory, for now, it was just dull. Perhaps a bit tense—par for the course for a bunch of underdogs chasing their luck and various mad rumors on top of each other in a small town.

Noll sighed and scanned the room again. She was restless, and she didn't like it. That was usually Jayce's thing. The fruit and flower still lives, seaside landscapes, and flickering holo-images of gigantic spaceships gawked at her from the walls judgingly. Even the quiet jazz that filtered out from hidden loudspeakers, competing with the noise of the storm outside, bothered her.

She ruffled up the short black locks that smoothed, uncomfortably sticky, onto the top of her head. Either something interesting happened soon or she was out of here, fast. They had enough to do back on Metallia. The machine shop didn't stock itself up, and their clients weren't waiting around for them to finish up with their whimsical escapades.

"Hey, you." Noll flinched at the voice, but it was just Saori Hamilton, the innkeeper, stopping beside her table and peering at her face from behind elegant glasses. "All done for today?"

Noll pushed her plate away. "Yeah. Thanks for the grub. Nice crowd tonight, huh?"

Saori patted the sides of her overall, wiping something off her hands. "Sure is."

"Still got that gun behind the bar?"

"And a couple of knives under the apron."

Noll grinned politely. The two of them had never been friends, but Jayce and Noll happened on Duplex often enough throughout the years that they'd gotten to know Saori a little. Not to mention the twins had enlisted the help of her uncle Wallace many times. With his communicating through lanes, weird tracking machines, and connections all over inhabited space, Wal's was a valuable friendship to cultivate.

But because Saori had also been part of those galaxy-changing events recently, Noll felt wary of engaging with her now. Not that the innkeeper was ever the bragging type—on the contrary. And maybe that was worse.

"It's not that bad," Saori went on. "Most of these travelers are more curious than dangerous. We'd become something of a meeting point here."

Noll followed the woman's glance towards the back of the room. Beside the travel-weary but always raucous lanehunters and quieter locals, even a blue-gray skinned, lean Nefirn turned up tonight, the air-converter embedded in their throat clearly identifying them if the faint scales on their arms didn't. In the other corner, three female helauns sat hunched under hefty chitinsacks talking to two Talalans whose solemn faces were crisscrossed by gray webbing similar to the veins of leaves.

Well. If you looked at it in a certain light, there *was* something nice about all these different people sitting together, getting to know each other, and exchanging information. Presumably plotting criminal activities. Noll smirked. The thought did nothing to subdue her jitters, though.

"What about her?" She subtly nodded towards a young woman of smaller stature sitting at a table close to the back wall. Taciturn and focused, Noll had seen the stranger in The Candle every day since they'd arrived. Never talking to anyone but not leaving either. Waiting. Watching like a hawk from under her straight-cut bangs, her neat braid glued to her shoulder like she was a doll, every movement calculated and careful.

Noll pulled her red jacket tighter around her. She was pretty sure the woman was a Union ex-agent.

"Oh, yeah. She's an ex-agent," Saori said casually.

Noll's eyes widened, her mouth suddenly parched. *Great. Awesome.* "And it doesn't bother you?"

"Not until she does something untoward. But she converses coherently and hasn't stirred any shit, so she isn't one of the more badly brainwashed." Saori frowned at Noll. "Why, want me to tie her up, get those knives out?"

THROUGH A WINDOW DARKLY

"I was just—"

"You're this jumpy about that guy, too?"

The woman inclined her head towards the lone Nefirn at the table in front of the window, staring out into the storm. Noll had seen them before, too. The fellow had arrived with a whole ship packed with their kin a few days ago. Nefirns had probably suffered the worst of the Union's flogging—it made sense that they were now trickling out to look around in the galaxy for the first time in long decades. This one was always alone but still better at mingling than the rest of their compatriots who hadn't even stuck their noses out of their gigantic vessel yet, as far as Noll noticed.

"And what about that one?"

A tall, serious figure sat in the other corner: short, dark hair, jawline to cut your breakfast bread with, and stern brown eyes under fuzzy eyebrows. Noll heard his name thrown around by the locals. Temak. Not much more than that, though.

"What is he?" she asked.

"Net."

Ooh, a handsome rebel. "Safe enough, I guess."

Saori clicked her tongue. "You'd think that."

Noll rolled her eyes. *So condescending.* But to be fair, Temak didn't exactly look like the happy, accomplished spy Noll expected someone whose organization had recently managed to destroy the Union's hegemony over the galaxy to be.

Perhaps he'd lost someone. Lots had.

She reached up to sweep the hair out of her eyes. "Are you trying to convince me this posse is dangerous or that they're not?"

Saori leaned down for the plate and cutlery on Noll's table. "Neither. Only that you shouldn't judge too fast. That's kinda what did us in the last time."

Noll huffed. "I said it was a nice crowd. And I'm not the one with those knives on my belt."

"No, you're the one with the blaster on your belt."

Ugh. Whatever.

Saori began to walk away with the dirty dishes but spun back after a second. She sighed, pulling her mouth to an apologetic smile. "Sorry. Didn't mean to school you. Clearly, I'm tense. Not sure why, it's an evening like any other."

Noll swallowed. She was familiar with that feeling, even though she wouldn't have admitted it. Particularly not to Saori. "As I always say. Can't hurt to be careful," she replied only.

Saori smiled again. "See you around, Noll."

Noll leaned back in her chair with a small snort as the woman walked away. Saori *was* worried, no matter how much she tried hiding it. Her vindication was overshadowed by the nervous jitter in the middle of her chest she knew so well. It had been there her whole life.

The distant thunder and persistent bellow of the wind outside echoed the uncomfortable sensation inside her. The world had always been a mess. It had been space pirates versus looming, oppressive galactic empire (sprinkled with mostly outsider alien worlds and a few independent human planets) for so long that people had gotten used to it. And sure, the universe was better off without the Union clenching an iron fist around its subjugated solar systems, but with it falling apart, the usual power balance was gone. The scattered fractions of humanity, be it scavenging, smuggling lanehunters, scheming resistances like the Net, or independent worlds like Miyoza, separated by distance, time, and differences in survival methods, now desperately hustled for any little morsel that could give them an advantage. And perhaps help them fill that Union-shaped vacuum, too.

All of us, survivors of a universe-sized catastrophe, scrambling to stay alive. And amidst this turmoil, the lanes, more resembling cracks on the walls of The Candle rather than capricious spacetime tunnels, continued to shine their foggy blue light on the creations of sentients, filling their hearts with awe and fear. In their shadows, the charred ruins of hundreds and thousands of abandoned, dead worlds looked upon it all with void eyes. A reminder of the fragility of reality and the most grotesque joke played on intelligent species: that the same phenomenon—the formation of lanes—causing the destruction of those civilizations ended up opening the universe for the survivors of the cataclysm. Sources of riches and danger, highways for transport, back doors for the renegade, checkpoints for the despot—the lanes were a constant. Unavoidable. And people kept living with them, doing the best and worst they could.

Noll shivered. Yeah, she kept living. Skies knew she tried.

The storm raged on outside, piling gray clouds on the darkening sky. Noll imagined the rain sweeping over the puddle-ridden main streets of Blackbones, the lightning strikes streaking along the surface of the gigantic vertical expanse of the Window on the outskirts of town. She knew that in contrast with the heavy rainclouds here, many times the skies of Duplex-2 looked clear through the gateway, making the sight even more eerie.

Maybe when it got quieter out there, she'd wander out. Maybe.

There was another bolt of lightning, and this time, distant shouting mixed with the thunder. Or was she hearing it wrong? No, others in the room were also twisting their heads around, looking through the windows, searching for the source. Behind the bar, Saori's frown deepened.

They didn't have to wait long for answers. The entrance of The Candle flew open, and a man leaned in, his work uniform soaked through and dripping a sizeable puddle onto the tiled floor.

"Gravsurf performance at the Window, now!" he yelled out with a wide grin. "World record attempt! Come on, everyone!"

And he was off, throwing himself into the storm again. The shouting continued outside, and Noll glimpsed several running figures in the pouring rain, trailing the first guy towards the east. Towards the Window.

HELYNA L. CLOVE

The dining crowd didn't have to be told twice. People jumped up, bumping into each other and pushing others out of the way to escape into the deluge. Even short-term visitors knew the Krotke twins and their infamous "gravsurf world record attempts".

Noll rose, stretching her limbs hastily, awake and ready at once. Gravsurf might be something worthy to sink her time in until Jayce got back from wherever he'd fucked off to. Hells, maybe she'd find him there. Getting drenched in a horrible gale sucked, but getting drenched in a horrible gale while watching Ruis and Rolte attempt to off themselves again?

Now, that was kinda cool.

2

Noll clambered towards the entrance of The Candle, moving with the crowd like with the tide, but before she could surface in the outside air, she halted, inducing a wave of indignant grunts from those around her. Disregarding the mass of people doing their best to jostle past, she planted herself on the spot and fished out an excitedly vibrating tablet from her jacket pocket.

A message from Jayce flashed up. *"Get your butt over here, stupid. It's party time!"*

As expected, he was already there, probably knee-deep in the mud of No Man's Land, the stretch of barren terrain leading to the Window. The attached photo showed his grinning face lit by distant lights, with something that looked like an elevated platform behind him in the distance.

A group chat notification popped up next. Jayce was inviting her, a couple of locals, and several Window-guards to a betting game, and speculations were already rolling in. Rolte would break his middle finger again; Ruis would end up on the other side, and county patrol would need to get him from the afars' custody like last time; both of them would crash and burn after five minutes with all their equipment totaled. No, after ten minutes. Or, according to the brave guess of another challenger, the twins would actually finish their performance, and even their fancy outfits might survive the trials.

Noll suppressed a chuckle and typed in her own bet: seven and a half minutes, only light bruising. No matter how much she loved to taunt the Krotkes—this town was not big enough for two pairs of twins, after all—she respected them. Their persistence alone was admirable.

She wasn't betting too many doubloons on them, though. She didn't trust anyone that much; no one but Jayce. Plus, she wasn't swimming in money.

Lunging forward again, she almost managed to slip out under the darkening sky when someone stopped in front of *her* this time. She collided with the figure with vigorous momentum, both of them losing their balance, and Noll would have certainly landed on the ground if she didn't catch the stranger's arm the last second. She also stepped on their foot while doing that, like, twice.

The person, a Nefirn, hissed in pain. People around them kept pushing through, so Noll circled the poor soul, pulling them with her out of the direct cross-section of the door, only vaguely registering that their gaze was cloudy like they weren't entirely present.

"Fuck, sorry, man," she muttered and stopped. What if she'd hurt the Nefirn more than she thought? "You alright?"

The alien looked like they wanted to answer but couldn't, and also like they wanted to burst into tears the next second. They had no time for either, because Saori popped into existence beside the two of them and placed a firm hand on the Nefirn's shoulder. "Are you okay, Liepok?"

The Nefirn succeeded at a whispered, meek "yes". Noll rolled her eyes.

"That's exactly what I asked!" she huffed. But nothing had even happened. Nefirns weren't made of glass last time she checked.

She recognized them in the meantime. It was the one that always loitered alone in The Candle, the one Saori had pointed out for her.

"Noll Morgan." The innkeeper turned to her just when Noll decided to split. Most of the people had already cleared out of the room and were halfway to the Window. *Damn. They're gonna hog the best spots!*

"What?" she barked back. Nothing in their previous conversation had given her the impression that Saori was this Nefirn's self-appointed

THROUGH A WINDOW DARKLY

bodyguard, but, of course, the woman had always been all about saving the weak and whatnot. "I said I was sorry!"

Saori sighed. She stepped back behind the bar to pull out a black raincoat and looped it around her lean form. The Nefirn just stood there with that same expressionless face like they'd been enchanted.

Noll didn't move either. Her mood soured, and it'd barely had time to turn sweeter. This was exactly why she didn't talk to Saori more than she had to. She tended to bring the impudent little kid out of her, and she wasn't even that much older than Noll! Ten years? Eight? *Bet it's not more than five. Ridiculous.* The innkeeper started moving again, rushing to the open door, and she turned back to the Nefirn and her with a patient smile. "So. What are we waiting for?"

The wind sprayed a cloud of prickly raindrops against Noll's neck. The Nefirn—Liepok—finally shifted, inching around her and keeping their distance painstakingly while they followed Saori into the night.

Right. Guess we're going together.

"How come you're leaving the pub?" the Nefirn asked Saori as Noll caught up to them. Her tablet vibrated again: Jayce was sending new photos. There wasn't a whole lot to see on the first, especially because his finger covered a quarter of the view—the most she could make out were rainbow-colored lights throwing their smudgy illumination on a mass of people treading mud, and that stage or platform, somewhat closer than before. The sky seemed brighter than the ground as light scattered on raindrops, and looming behind everything, like a billowy water surface turned perpendicular to the terrain, there was the Window.

The second photo was Jayce's round face sticking out a tongue at her. The flash made his skin look brilliant white. *Idiot boy.*

Meanwhile, Saori gave a shrug at Liepok's question. "Bernard will keep an eye out. He's my assistant. Something tells me I'll be needed out there."

Noll rolled her eyes again. Self-appointed bodyguard *and* peacekeeper. Saori was taking herself way too seriously these days. Sure, she'd always put the rowdy types into their places in and around The Candle, and it wasn't like that was a bad thing, but...

This is different. For some reason. She's so full of herself sometimes.

She suppressed her frustration, but the Nefirn was drinking up Saori's every word with a glint of adoration in their eyes. It annoyed her. A lot. But before she could have commented on it, they arrived at an intersection that turned them onto the road leading out of town and to the Window.

Mud squelched under their boots in the wide cracks of the broken concrete as they walked, and through the curtain of rain on both sides, dark buildings emerged like visions. From time to time, the white flash of a lightning burned the contours of people and objects into Noll's retinas with the crackling, booming sound of thunder arising at the same time. The lightning strikes seemed to come from ahead, from behind the last buildings at the edge of town.

Saori launched into explaining gravsurf to the Nefirn just when they stepped out from between the houses and abruptly found themselves in No Man's Land. The sky was completely dark by then, rain suffocated living and inanimate both, and the sludge under their feet climbed up their shins. Several dozen, mostly humanoid figures hurried about the soggy wasteland, crowding in the direction of floodlights in the distance, trying to yell over the thunder and deluge as they went. Flashlights and tablets threw their bluish light onto faces human and otherwise—tiny stars in the night. Noll gazed ahead where colorful beacons framed a wide stage like at a concert or circus show, and the pale beams of floodlights swung back and forth from the crowd to the Window and back again.

Those lights were the only reason the gigantic vertical surface towering above them was visible. Like liquid glass or disturbed pond water as far as the eye could see, the gateway extended, separating the

THROUGH A WINDOW DARKLY

dark skies of Duplex-1 and Duplex-2. It was a triangular tear in the air when seen from space but far too wide to glimpse all borders of it from this close up. It was also too dark now on both planets to properly make out the other side except for the shadows of trees and maybe houses in the distance—only the fluctuating interface was there, a chaotic pattern in the air and something not quite right with the perspective. If one was orbiting the planet on a ship (and good luck doing that) it would have looked like the two planets were conjoined twins, stuck to each other along the plane of this hazy-edged but stable hole in the tapestry of space-time.

Well, stable. Noll snorted to herself. If daily tempests and brutal gravitational instabilities could be included in the expression, then sure. And there was also the very, *very* unsettling phenomenon where one could see nothing when approaching the Window from the other direction. No interdimensional crossing except some weird shimmer in the air and gravity going bananas.

After the first exodus from Old Earth, the people eventually becoming lanehunters had found Duplex relatively quickly, and they'd been holding it ever since if one could believe the messy documentation that remained from those early times. The Union had never truly fought for it—more trouble to control than it was worth—and since the weather and physical anomalies made it hard to maintain any kind of elaborate headquarters on the planets, Duplex had historically been the site of temporary, shady hideouts and irregular raids, if anything at all. Mostly, it was home to little towns, some struggling agriculture, and a whole lot of mud.

Noll left Saori and the Nefirn behind and veered to the right on a quest to find Jayce. Going by his photos, she must have been close to him now, but she couldn't pick him out of the crowd yet. Then she could barely see anything anymore, because suddenly, more lights emerged around the stage area, blinding everyone, and triumphant music boomed forth from somewhere.

The crowd parted as two figures marched through it to take their place in the wreath of lights on the stage, their backs at the wide expanse of the Window.

People cheered, shouted, and clapped. Noll couldn't help but grin as well. *What theatrical nonsense.* Even worse than the last time she'd seen them. Further colorful lights blinked on around the stage, throwing thin beams onto the Window. The surface seemed more disturbed now, bubbling like a pot of boiling water. The crowd pushed forward; red-uniformed Window-guards walked the edges and yelled out for everyone to be careful with little effect. Noll fought her way closer to the stage, still searching. The Krotkes must have gotten intel about a forecasted grav instability from the guards, disseminated the news among the locals, and then waited in one of the guard posts for the first waves to appear. The forecasting system wasn't especially accurate, but those rickety machines could at least tell a few hours ahead that a larger event was coming.

The twins stood in the center of the lights, enjoying the applause. Every inch of their white coveralls was filled with string lights, mirrors, and reflective metallic plates with small cogs, wiring, and pieces of machinery on strategic places complicating the setup. From their backs, wings made of an iridescent, spiderweb-fine material sprung forth and billowed to the ground. As they spun around, showing themselves off, their wings jittered, but Noll knew the movement had little to do with the gusts of wind in the chilly air.

The thin sheets lifted up and up in a spiralling motion and then extended and crescented out in a wide arc above the twins' heads. Ruis struck a pose like a model, grinned widely, and spread his arms out. The next moment, both brothers lifted off from the ground and shot out towards the dark sky.

The floodlights attempted to follow them but weren't fast enough. The two men shrunk to darkened spots above, and Noll saw nothing but the straight-line trajectories of raindrops and the simmering surface of the Window while the music, orchestrated to drums and whining guitars, thumped faster and faster. People whooped in a frenzy. Lightning zapped through the Window's surface in a large arc, drowning everything in light. Nothing of Duplex-2 could be seen now, and only some dark earth and dark sky loomed through the chaotically bubbling surface, but Noll imagined the spectators on the other side anyway: the afars leaning on the walls of their tidy stone houses, watching. Those guys had always been more outlandish about their rules and regulations around the Window, but even they couldn't deny a Krotke-show.

Then the twins returned, first as small glimmering points above, then plummeting towards the stage with wings swirling and outfits glittering. Their arms were bent as if they were fiddling around with the devices built into their clothes as they dropped, and that was exactly what was happening. They were making quick adjustments on their gear to modify their velocity and direction—the whole thing sounded very scientific whenever they tried to explain it, but whatever they were doing, it made them able to ride the wildly dancing gravitational waves around the Window. They were swimming, dancing in the storm.

They stopped mid-air, floating sideways and in a circle, floundering like fish in the ocean. Raindrops rose from the ground towards the skies around them; pebbles, globules of water, and pieces of muddy earth lifted up nearby in the upside-down-turned gravitation. A light beam flared around violently: it had been torn from the ground, and two Window-guards were trying to pull it back down by its cables. Colors flashed and reflected from the twins' outfits and the thousands of waterdrops clinging to the fabric—they looked like dragonflies now, two fragile creatures in war with the elements.

One wrong move or slow reaction was enough, and they were no more than a blotch of flesh and broken bones on the ground.

Noll tore her eyes off their mesmerizing, deadly dance. She still couldn't see Jayce. She shot him a message. *Hope your view is good, stupid.*

As she turned back towards the stage, a strange feeling encroached her. She hadn't looked at who she'd drifted next to in the crowd before, but following the itch, she wiped the water off her face and glanced to the side. First, she thought it was Liepok again because they were so tall—but no, their hair was darker and their clothes different, not the grey coveralls. The woman stood rigidly beside her as if at attention, her face tense in wild contrast with the mass of people going apeshit over the Krotke's performance. And—because Noll could sniff this out in total darkness—a plasma blaster's grip was sticking out from her belt behind the nondescript coat.

The Union ex-agent from The Candle.

Noll clenched her fingers into a fist and took a step away from the woman. She shifted her eyes back to the flying twins. *Damn agents. Should be banned from Duplex.* Brainwashed or not, they were unreliable. Who knew which of them served Leadership, only pretending to be rogue? Who knew what Leadership was even doing these days? Sure, it had said it would stand down. Sure, it was now apparently re-thinking its life or whatever. *Doubt it.* What if it was still trying to infiltrate, annex new places, rebuild its lost empire? Yes, people kept bumping into Union deserters—like Saori had not long ago—who were, allegedly, well-meaning, but it was no reason to embrace all of them thoughtlessly.

These agents had been keeping the galaxy in terror for the last couple hundred years. Those eager to forget and forgive should ask Liepok and their people, forced into servitude, locked up on their planets and forgotten by all, whether that was fair. *Bet they wouldn't be so eager to give amnesty.*

The performance went on. Ruis and Rolte showed off their sweeping air-acrobatics while the music throbbed and the lights pulsed,

THROUGH A WINDOW DARKLY

but Noll couldn't enjoy it anymore. Not with the danger this close. Nervous foreboding sat in her stomach, and the memories of a different kind of booming sound echoed across her body. Flashing lights on a rain-drenched street. Hard Union boots stomping on wet concrete, neon signs flickering, screams and shouts in the distance. Explosions, close-by. Too close. Huddling behind a flimsy door, quiet, so quiet, begging soundlessly it would pass, *oh, please, let it pass.*

A loud *crack* echoed off the stage. Noll shook herself. Cold sweat sat on her brow. Another *groan*, immense like an old god waking in the core of the planet. Nothing the people of Blackbones hadn't heard before—this often occurred when the grav waves started prying the rock layers up and against each other under the ground. The Window-guards must have been seconds away from cancelling this whole shebang. The Krotke twins wrote vigorous spirals in the air above everyone's heads, releasing fireworks from their loony outfits, maybe in preparation for a grand finale.

Noll squinted to the side. The agent—ex-agent—had disappeared. The crowd swayed back and forth around her, awe and wonder sparkling potently in the air. Her eyes shifted towards the stage and to the right where the flood of light met muddy darkness, and—finally!

Jayce's blonde mop of hair shone through the dim like a blob of energized plasma. He bobbed up and down in excitement, the bright green stripe on his jacket reflecting the light in a familiar flash of color. He was watching the show in a loose circle of Nefirns, somewhat separately from the main crowd.

Huh. Even those guys had come out to watch this madness. *Gravsurf really brings people together.*

Another *bang* rattled the landscape. Bit noisier than usual, wasn't it? But no one reacted; the dramatics just fired up the mood further. The guards would have taken action if things got more dangerous than expected, right?

HELYNA L. CLOVE

She wasn't looking at the Window when it happened. She was watching Jayce and the Nefirns, engaged in banter judging from the cheeky grin on her twin's face. He must have dragged them into his bets. Noll was about to check her tablet for a message when one of the Nefirns lifted a spindly arm and pointed at the Window. They stumbled backward, colliding with the group of their associates. Jayce spun around, too, but Noll didn't have time to glimpse what it was that spooked him.

A bright flare of light flooded No Man's Land. The vast surface of the Window had turned into a brilliant mirror, a shard reflecting nothing but pure white. Noll's eyes closed shut on their own accord, and she raised both her hands in front of her to block out the glow.

Her guts twitched. That glare was familiar. White-blue like the radar screens of the *Taro* when Noll skated too close to a lane barrier.

Like the insides of a lane.

Someone collided with Noll. Then someone else. She opened her eyes, stumbling, half-blinded. The crowd was retreating from the terrifying light, and above them all, the Window was bursting apart, fog pouring out, the brilliance unbearable.

She staggered backwards. *This isn't possible.* The Window didn't do this. It had never done anything like this before.

Someone shouted, "Everyone back off!" Maybe a Window-guard. The mass of people jostled against Noll, shouts welling up, the panic cresting and washing over her. Feet and sharp elbows pushed against her; rain drenched her; there was barely any air in her lungs. She lost Jayce, lost the Window itself—there was nothing but bodies in desperate flight and that blue light penetrating skin and bones. Her heart fluttered like a trapped moth, limbs numb as she tried to flee and swim against the tide at the same time.

Jayce...

But the tide was strong; she wasn't making any progress. There was another deep rumble, and earth-shaking screams answered it in a cacophony of voices. Then the blue glare cut off as suddenly as it had come.

A force, a hurricane rising from nothing, grabbed Noll and slammed her to the ground. Pain blossomed at the nape of her neck, all tension released, and the world went void.

When she woke with the sound of a discordant bell tolling inside her head, she knew she hadn't been out for long. Her skull felt heavy, but when she clambered to her knees in the sludge spitting out bitter muck and blades of soggy grass, something started ticking in her brain.

She needed to find Jayce. She needed to make sure he was okay.

It was still dark. Still raining. The sea of mud under her had gotten worse; hundreds of sticky tentacles tried to drag her down by the boots as she pushed herself up. The crowd had dispersed—she saw only a few figures stagger around in the faint illumination of the distant street lamps. But she couldn't focus because the next moment her glance climbed the Window, and—

The night landscape of Duplex-2 had disappeared, and instead, there was the blackness of space. Stars sprinkled on dark canvas. Nothingness without a planet to tether it.

Wait, what? Is this a joke? Where was Duplex-2? What the fuck was happening?

"Hey, are you okay?" A figure stopped beside her, their contours solidifying. Noll squinted at them through the ache gripping her skull and the large raindrops clinging to her eyelashes. It was Saori's Nefirn, Liepok. They were limping, their arms muddy up to the elbow.

"Yeah." Noll grabbed the hand the alien offered to balance herself for a second. "What— How did this happen?" Her voice was shaky, the Window pulling her gaze once again. *How is this possible. How?*

The Nefirn's words reached her through a gale of blood buzzing in her ears. "I don't...I don't know. I'm looking for my friends. Did you see where they went?"

Noll couldn't answer. A tightness constricted her chest, the impossible stars through the Window hanging silently above her. The plane of divide was sharp—on this side, turbulent dark clouds, on the other, pinprick-sharp diamond-scatter into infinity. There was nothing else. Duplex-2 had vanished. The Window seemed to lead somewhere else now.

Jayce had been standing too close. Too close to whatever had gone down.

The ticking in her mind became a screaming alarm. She lurched forward, fighting through the gunk towards where she'd last seen him. The wet earth was broken up there, overturned like a ship had just taken off of it. She could make out the stage and the blinded floodlights nearby in the darkness. The metallic platform was askew, nearly flipped over; the Krotkes were nowhere to be found. The Nefirns were gone. And Jayce was gone, too.

Maybe they just ran away fast. Maybe that's all.

But Jayce would be here, looking for her. She fished the tablet out of her jacket pocket. There were no new messages.

"What the fuck happened?" she asked again, turning back to the Nefirn who had followed her like a quiet shadow. "Have you seen something? Where...where's the fucking planet? Where's Duplex-2?"

Where's my brother?!

"I..."

"I saw what happened." Noll whipped around at the new voice. The guy standing a few feet away from her with his face mostly in shadow was familiar, but she couldn't place him for a second.

THROUGH A WINDOW DARKLY

The person beside him, though, she recognized instantly. The ex-agent woman glared at her, tension stretching every muscle on her face.

"Out with it then!" Noll snapped at the man whose name she'd forgotten.

He didn't look at her; he was staring at the Window like he saw ghosts drifting along its strange surface. "I stood farther away so it didn't reach me. There was...that blue glare, and some another place appeared through the Window. Not Duplex-2. Then another, and another. Different planets, different locations, I think? Then it was like something came out of it, the Window itself was swelling and overflowing. Your friends,"—he nodded towards Liepok and finally caught Noll's eyes—"they couldn't get away in time. The anomalous effect pulled them through. The twins, too."

Tiny white stars surged into an ever-moving spiral in front of Noll's eyes. Dizziness sprouted in her core, cold buzz twisting around her fingers. She needed to sit down.

No, wait. Not that. She had to move. She had to move, *now*. But she couldn't.

"We need to know what happened to the afars," the agent woman spoke up. "Whether they experienced the same thing."

"County patrol must be already on their way," the man replied, glancing at the comms device on his wrist and then towards town. "They'll contact Duplex-2, figure out what's going on."

There was no crowd of rescuers or researchers gathering yet, but he might have been right. Temak, Noll realized distantly. That was his name. The handsome Net spy.

"My crew...my friends..." Liepok made a small, painful sound. "The captain..."

No tears rolled down their cheeks—Noll wasn't even sure Nefirns could cry—but their body trembled, their tone desolate. The Net guy shut his mouth. The implications rumbled through all of them.

Noll's heart was beating so hard she thought it might just crash through her ribs. She still couldn't move, but maybe it was good. Maybe then time wouldn't, either. Maybe then she could unmake all of this.

No. No, no, no. She shook herself and blinked out the stupor. That wasn't gonna work. That was not nearly good enough.

Her arm shot out on its own volition, clawing into the Net operative's shoulder. "When did they get pulled through?" she croaked.

The man twisted away, indignant, and from the corner of her eyes, Noll saw the agent's hand move towards her belt. That made her hold onto the guy even harder. "Before or after the Window changed to its current state?"

Temak searched her face. Empathy and aloof confusion mixed in his glance. Then uncertainty. "I'm not sure. After, I think? When it stopped switching."

Noll let him go. Okay. Okay, that's good. Bad, terrible, but good.

Because if they'd gotten pulled through after, then she could follow. And even though there was nothing but outer space through the gateway now, Jayce had to be wearing the compact spacesuit they'd swiped from that Rixian con man months ago. He had to wear it under his clothes, because Noll was wearing it, too. And if he'd reacted fast enough, he could have gotten the helmet on before he suffocated. The oxygen tank in it was enough for a little more than...two hours? Maybe? If the diverter didn't fail like last time.

She looked at the Window again. The surface was perfectly transparent glass now, and through it, the void blinked back at her. Whatever had happened to it might happen again. She could lose her chance any minute.

The *Taro* was docked on the other side of town. She had to be fast.

Spinning on her heels, she was ready to start running, but she didn't get far. The Union agent grabbed her arm and held her firmly in place. "You're going through. You can't go alone."

Noll snapped her arm away. "You can't tell me what I can't do," she seethed.

"Maybe it's better to wait for the patrol," Liepok muttered. "I'm sure they'll start an organized search. Who knows what's through there?"

Noll backed away. There was no time! "No, I'm going now."

"I'm with you." Temak stepped up beside her. There was sympathy in his eyes; he must have guessed Noll had personal reasons. "We'll find them."

The agent released an exasperated grunt. "Not a chance." It looked like she was suppressing an eye-roll, and then looked at Noll with a diamond-hard stare. "But you can use *me*."

Noll nearly burst out in laughter. As if she'd take a Union agent she'd rather drown in a spoonful of water with her!

Liepok, probably emboldened by Temak's motivation, moved beside the Net spy. "If you think we can do something...I'm coming with." Their voice was barely above a terrified whisper, their face frozen.

Noll blinked. Stars, none of this mattered. She was out of there, and now.

"You're with me." She pointed at the Nefirn. Then at Temak. "And you. Let's go." And she was off, sprinting back to town.

3

"I gotta mention...we don't really know...what we're up against," Temak heaved as he trailed her. The Nefirn was keeping pace, too, but they'd left the Union agent behind a few minutes ago. "There's just empty space through there. Do you think—"

"I'm not *thinking* anything," Noll retorted. She flew through the streets at top speed, around and among people slowly drifting back towards the Window. On one of the main streets, a group of patrol people ran past them. "My brother might be out there in that empty space, so I'm not thinking about much of anything until I find him. Understood?"

That shut him up. Noll blinked tears and rain out of her eyes. *Hurry, hurry, hurry.* It wasn't too late yet.

She was a small hurricane, navigating the shortest route through Blackbones towards the spacedocks, and then sweeping through the wide-open entrance of the main dome of the docks. The couple of workers on duty cleared out of her way in short order as she flashed her tablet where she needed to and headed down the accelways of the atrium. Temak and Liepok were close behind her.

She counted the seconds. It had taken her around ten minutes to cross town—she could have swiped a shuttle somewhere, but it might have cost her time, so she'd rather relied on her quick feet. Patrol might be already busy setting up a blockade back in No Man's Land alongside the Window-guards, bringing in clan scientists, but if she was fast, she could slip through. As the ungainly grey mass of the *Taro* appeared sandwiched between two large Metallian freighters in Hangar C, she exhaled forcefully. Just a few minutes now. A finger jab on her tablet brought the ship's shields down and engaged the ramp for her to climb into the airlock. She clambered through the hatch and stomped along the corridor to the cockpit, shaking water off her clothes while the *Taro* flickered to life around her.

She tried not to think about air. About Jayce's dwindling oxygen. About how scared he must be, maybe hurt. About what was happening to the Window, where exactly the gateway was leading now, and what might end up separating her from her brother. She flopped into the pilot seat, the other two buckling up beside her. Sealing the ship and spinning up the engines, she fired a request to lift off and did so before she even received authorization.

Her tablet vibrated. She glanced at it in passing. It was Saori.

"Where are you? Are you two okay? Where are you going?"

So, she'd seen her. Noll swiped away the message. She had no time to explain.

"We're good to go," Temak reported from the co-pilot seat, staring at his tablet. He was making himself useful. *Good.* "A couple of frigates have lifted off from Cuiran, but they're not there yet. Judging by their chatter, the Window seems to be doing weird things again."

Fuck. They were running out of time. Noll steered the *Taro* out of the hangar, heading north. It took mere seconds—she was flying as fast as she dared—and skirting closer, she immediately saw what Temak was talking about. The gigantic, triangular gateway looming above the landscape showed the same starry expanse as before, but its surface was in motion, fluctuating like a thin membrane tapped by an enormous finger, waves breezing over it again and again.

Noll aimed the *Taro's* nose at the wobbling stars. With the Window leading into space, it looked like someone stabbed a huge, darkened knife into the evening landscape—around it, sparkling alien space melted into sparkling local space. Shivers ran down her back. She'd crossed lanes a thousand times; she'd crossed the Window as well. But nothing was normal about this. They could be dead the moment they made contact.

THROUGH A WINDOW DARKLY

"It's still leading to the same place," Liepok whispered behind her. Noll felt them clutching at the back of her chair, the spongy material depressing from the movement. "We can save them."

Liepok's crew had not looked like they were wearing spacesuits, but who knew. Maybe their bodies could take the low pressure and complete lack of breathable substances for a while. Or the Nefirn was just grasping at straws because they had to. Like Noll.

Blackness encroached the screens. There were no other ships around, no one preparing to go on a rescue mission yet. No one hailed them or tried to stop them as the *Taro* approached the boundary. The starry sky filled their view, and fleetingly, Noll thought about how they perhaps should have searched for more information before running into the unknown, or considered their options better. Saori or her uncle could have helped…or the Net…fuck, even that damn agent—but then gravity pivoted, her stomach did a nauseating cartwheel, and there was no turning back anymore.

Crossing lanes sucked. Keeping your ship on a vector while the rising temperature and pressure crunched and twisted the hull, and exotic radiation bit chunks off whatever organic matter it fancied the most; the constant danger of falling into the void or getting lost millions of light-years away from your target if you veered just a hair off the stable path; that last moment when the upside-down, inside-out space-time phased back into normal, the reference systems tangled together and drifted apart, and everything inside you held a breath, praying you stayed alive. And granted, you mostly did if reasonably prepared, but the body felt it every time. The mind as well, no matter what lanehunters told themselves. If you crossed too often, your very essence was at risk.

This crossing was a hundred times worse than any Noll had experienced before.

The *Taro* plummeted through the boundary, and the moment stretched into infinity. Her bones turned liquid; the blood halted in her veins. Her eyeballs dried out, stuck to the lids, the view ahead sharpening, crystallizing, then with a sigh, all form and solidity peeled away. For a split second, the fragile barrier between her and the outside world dissolved, her skin gossamer-light, fragile shell that couldn't possibly shield her from the burning, gaping gashes of eternity.

Her thoughts slowed. Her heart skipped a beat. Two beats. Three. Everything—stopped.

For a long, achingly long second, she was nothing.

Then she slammed back in, colliding with time and space like the *Taro* with concrete on a rickety landing platform. Back in her body, back in rigid reality.

The vibrations registered first, the spaceship's thrusters adapting output to the changed environmental parameters. Then the noise: the rattling of the hull and the whine of the engine as it tried to keep them flying even. Noll held onto the dashboard, blinking, hands shaking, alien in the space she called home. *I'm here. I'm still here. I'm alive.*

The feeling dissipated, a bad vision. Noll inhaled. It smelled like oil around her, and she closed her eyes for a second. It always smelled like oil on the *Taro*.

She threw a glance at her passengers, saw them gasp and brace themselves. "Everybody lucid and sane?" she asked. Temak and Liepok only answered with weak nods and grunts, but it was enough for now. Noll scanned the radar screens and decreased acceleration so the ship got out of the danger zone without drifting too far from the Window.

Her heart sprung into her throat. The instruments beeped about, indicating normal conditions outside, and there was nothing weird on the radars either. Wherever they were, it was same old, same old outer space. No planets, no suns in a million miles vicinity, only the Window in the middle of the void.

She directed the sensors at it, but even with her bare eyes she could see Duplex-1 through the wobbling, stormy surface. Milky white fog seeped out at the edges of the gateway. Temak rose from his seat he

THROUGH A WINDOW DARKLY

glared at the view with such intensity while Noll's fingers continued their dance on the keyboard, running short-range, sensitive scans, searching for debris in the vicinity.

Debris. Bodies.

There was nothing.

Temak looked at her. His tone was cautious when he started to speak. "Depending on initial speed, they could be farther out—"

"I know!" The air was tight in her chest. She sounded meaner than she intended to. "I know."

She closed her eyes. Inhaled. Considered kicking the dashboard to rubble or screaming as loud as she could. Then she opened her eyes, exhaled, and continued working.

A couple of minutes later, she launched a rudimentary algorithm that took the ship around the Window in circles with increasing radius and changing inclination to scan the region of space around them. The best way she could think of to go about this. She leaned back in the seat, spent. The *Taro's* short-range radar was able to sense a human body-sized object, for sure. If they were out here, she'd find them. It was the question of precious, precious time.

Well. Except, as Temak had said, depending on initial speed, they could be far, far away already. She didn't know what exactly happened as they got pulled through, after all. Noll might just circle out here like a lost bird, looking for something that was moving away from her faster than she could even notice.

"Hey." Temak's voice rang so uncertain that it made her tear her glance off the screens. But he wasn't talking to her. "How about you sit down now?"

The man rose, moving behind Noll where Liepok, having stood from the spare seat now leaned against the inner hull, shaking. Noll wasn't sure about what range of hues were natural for Nefirn skin, but the yellow-gray coloring of their scales was probably not indicative of nominal state. Liepok's eyes were glued to the starry sky on the main screen, their mouth half-open when Temak cautiously took them by the arm and guided them into the co-pilot seat.

"Do you want something to drink? Eat?" the man implored.

The Nefirn blinked and turned their head to stare at him, eyes unfocused. "Water...water would be great," they said weakly.

Temak glanced at Noll with a question in his eyes. It made frustration shoot into her stomach, and her eyes flitted back to the radar screen. She couldn't leave the instruments. At any moment, they might find her brother—

The cockpit pivoted to the side, and she grabbed the arm of the pilot seat. No sudden trajectory changes, she was just feeling dizzy. Water sounded nice, actually. The rational voice at the back of her head whispered that the search could take hours, and she'd get a ping on her tablet anyway if—*when, gods damnit,* when—something or someone was found. But until then, they needed to keep themselves alive.

"Don't touch anything," she grunted and climbed out of the pilot seat. She rushed out and down the hallway into the living compartment and scooped up two bottles of water and a couple of nutribars from the cupboard.

When she returned, Temak was asking questions again, crouched beside the Nefirn. "And what's your name?"

"Liepok." Their voice was shaky, eyes still clouded. The poor thing was hanging on by a very weak thread.

Temak saw it too. His tone rose a pitch in forced lightness. "Nice to meet you, Liepok. I'm Temak. Look, this screen here says the ship's name is *Taro*. Do you know what a taro is? It's like...a formless, brown root vegetable. Like potato. You know potato? It's similar but an uglier shape. Nutritious, though."

Liepok made a weak sound, not exactly a chuckle but something that could have been that on days better than this one. Their slender fingers held onto the seat like it was a lifeline. Temak took a water bottle from Noll, unscrewed the cap, and gave it to Liepok. They

THROUGH A WINDOW DARKLY

started gulping it down immediately, emptying it all out before taking the next breath. Noll was reminded that Nefirns usually drank salt water, the kind their oceans were made of back home. Their bodies automatically isolated and purged salt...or something similar. How did this clear water taste to Liepok now? Maybe it was disgusting. Not that Noll had salt water in storage. Although, maybe there was some in the—

She took a long inhale. She needed to focus. A glance at the radar screen confirmed they hadn't yet found zilch. Stars. This was going to be awful.

"Are you feeling better?" she asked, turning to the other two. Liepok nodded, and Temak eyed her with an enigmatic expression. She plopped back down into the pilot seat. "My name's Noll, by the way," she added. Introductions done now, finally.

Liepok's color definitely looked healthier. At least, Noll decided that blue-green had to be good.

"Why did you name your ship after an ugly root vegetable?" they asked.

Temak snorted, and Noll pulled her eyebrows into a frown. Then, a pang in her chest. *Because Jayce is an idiot, that's why.*

She couldn't say it. "I mean look at it." She shrugged. "Formless and ugly. But useful in a pinch."

Liepok's eyes glinted in what Noll hoped was humor, and Temak twisted his expression into an apologetic look, perhaps for calling her bird ugly. *Well, it was for a good cause.* She glanced at the radar screen again. Nothing.

Tick-tock, tick-tock.

Noll flung Temak and the Nefirn a nutribar each, but she didn't have the energy to start unwrapping hers. Tension vibrated at the back of her mind, a string pulled to tearing. She knew the feeling would not stop until they found something.

"We can't see them yet, right?" Liepok asked. Noll shook her head, and the Nefirn dropped their shoulders. "If they're out here...maybe it's already late."

"Maybe, maybe not," Temak said before Noll could snap at them. "Who is it for you?" he asked her.

An unexpected expected question. "My brother. Jayce," she managed to get out. "He's...he might be alive. He was in a suit. The twins' outfits should also keep them up for a while, if they were quick enough to realize what was happening. I think." *I think. I hope. I beg.*

"That's good," Liepok breathed. "That's very good."

"I've never seen a lane do something like this." The radar beeped empty. Noll really didn't want to listen to Temak's theories, but there was little else to do. He went on as if talking to himself. "When they form, sure. They say lane vectors and exits changed often and rapidly back then, even for the smaller ones. But lanes have been stable for hundreds of years. We know this. The Window has been doing its thing for centuries without fail. I don't...I don't understand."

"Maybe it was, um...caused intentionally?" Liepok wondered, munching on the nutribar. They seemed more present by the minute.

Temak cocked his head. "Maybe. Anything is possible, these days. But who? How and why?"

"Could be the clan scientists," Noll said, her voice hoarse. "They've been working on something. Maybe they fucked something up."

"Could also be Union. Some attempt that went wrong."

"Or right."

The two of them stared at each other, words running out. Terror froze the liquid in Noll's body to unyielding ice.

She looked at the radar screen. Nothing. It had roughly been fifteen minutes since they've crossed through. Around half an hour since Jayce had disappeared. Best case scenario, he had two hours of oxygen in his pack. If he kept it topped up. If the diverter was fine. *If, if, if...*

THROUGH A WINDOW DARKLY

"There was this machine," Liepok started. "I think it could do something like this. Funnel energy from lanes, open new ones. The Talalans—"

"I don't want to talk about it." Noll knew the story. Heard all the gossip. The war that had almost ended lanehunters, and then allegedly ended the Union. The Talalan device everyone had fought over. Destroyed since, if that could be believed. Saori had been there for the end. It was all so much bigger than Noll. "It doesn't matter what caused it. It happened."

"Perhaps it does matter," Temak said quietly, and Noll wanted to grumble at him that good gods, of course, it mattered, but did it matter *here* and *now*, but his tone was strangely sharp as he stared at the screens, and Noll had to follow his gaze.

Something was happening to the Window again. The triangular surface bubbled, bloating out and turning concave as if it was climbing wavefronts much larger-scale than itself. The edges of the gateway turned blurry behind the blue-white fog churning out of it like turbulent smoke.

Then the face of the gateway flickered. The curve of Duplex-1 that had still been visible through it disappeared like a screen turned off. There was nothing but darkness for a few seconds when the view suddenly popped back.

But it wasn't the planet Noll knew so well anymore. It was nothing. Void and stars.

The Window had changed exits again, and now, they were stuck.

Noll dropped her head into her palms, elbows propped on the dashboard. She'd been sitting there since forever, it felt like, although the computer kept insisting it had only been the better part of an hour. An hour of oxygen remained for Jayce, too, and Noll was getting exhausted by pretending her algorithm couldn't run without her. Temak had tried to get some food into her earlier, but she couldn't eat. She was glad for the big meal she'd had in the Candle.

The Candle. Blackbones. They'd barely left the place behind, but it all felt distant, in time and in space both. Who knew if she ever got back.

Who knew if she even would want to. Depending on what happened here.

She stopped herself. The Window could reset at any time. The radar could beep in a second, telling her Jayce was right outside, waiting for her to save him. Anything was possible. The universe was huge, and terrifying, and full of things Noll didn't understand, and as long as that was true, all of it was possible.

Jayce was alive. She would find him, and she would get them back home.

Even though the nav system had no clue in what gods-forgotten corner of the universe they were in. Constellations and quasar signals were unfamiliar in every direction so the computer couldn't place the *Taro* in its neat little galaxy box. It made no fucking sense; this never happened to her before. Could be that something smoked out in the system, but to be honest, Noll didn't want to think about it too deeply yet. The sharp pinpricks of stars glimmering all around—so many—seemed oppressive, confining, now.

There was also some weird radiation signal coming from the outer edges of the solar system they were in—weak but present in every direction. That scared her even more. They were so lost. Lost and alone against something she had no chance to see clearly.

THROUGH A WINDOW DARKLY

Shit. No. Jayce will know what to do. He always does. Always has a loony plan.

She found little success in trying not to torture herself wondering what Jayce would do smarter and better than her. What more he could possible come up with if he was in her place. Something that would be useful right now, some genius proposal that saved them all. But nothing came to mind. She was not Jayce. They were kindred but completely different. Certainly no extravagant plans were always at the ready in her head.

Restlessness tugged at her insides. Usually it was Jayce who couldn't sit on his buttocks, couldn't spend a day *being*. He wanted to be on the move, see things, do things, be a part of it all. If it was up to Noll, they would have still been stuck in the little machine shop their parents had left to them when they'd decided to fuck off into the unknown fourteen years ago with only one goodbye: *"Sorry, guys, we might not even come back, don't wait around for us."* This had never been a problem—at least that was what Noll kept telling herself—and admittedly, they'd done much more for their children than the average lanehunter. They'd been raised by the Totenhart clan after that. When they turned twenty, Jayce started muttering about how he wanted to go nomadic, and he just wouldn't stop, and obviously, Noll couldn't let him go alone. She couldn't lose someone else because she was too cowardly to follow them.

So, they'd become lanehunters. And it wasn't like Noll hated the life. It was usually chill, and they were good at it. Jayce planted and nourished connections and chose jobs with uncanny intuition, and Noll played the hard-ass, kept them in order, never letting themselves slip. They did everything together. Two against the world.

Against a chaotic, immense world which had no care about either of them. The world that might unravel at any moment, where the order of things could shift over the span of a night, where powers far above you routinely decided which side you were on in a battle you didn't know shit about. Where, if you trusted the wrong people, you were lost.

Of course, no one expected a lanehunter to change the ways of things or attempt heroics. Weren't they just glorified pirates, after all? The whole galaxy was theirs, they liked to say, which quelled the guilt in Noll's heart, usually. Maybe she was doing enough. Maybe it was fine to be afraid.

Then the talk of war and the fall of the Union reached them, alongside with gossip about those lanehunters who had brought it all upon the galaxy. Noll had complicated feelings about it, but she never imagined her involvement in those "big things" that always scared the hells out of her would start with losing the most important person in her life.

There was a polite cough from the back, and Temak stepped into the cockpit. His face was pale and gray but a bit more relaxed—or maybe just tired. He sat beside Noll in the co-pilot seat and offered her one of the mugs in his hands. "I heard you can blackmail any lanehunter with a cup of coffee."

Noll took the mug into her hands, the tendrils of warmth immediately driving the numb buzz from her bones. "Using my own coffee? I don't think it works like that, man."

Temak shrugged. "Worth a try."

"Why would you even want to blackmail me?"

"Insurance."

"Uh-huh." Noll leaned back and took a sip of coffee. Nice and strong, just how she liked it. "I take it you never worked with lanehunters before?" Considering his profession, it would have been weird, but maybe he'd only served on backwater worlds?

Unease and careful humor mixed on Temak's face. "Not with ones like you."

"What's that supposed to mean?"

THROUGH A WINDOW DARKLY

Temak hid behind his mug—the chipped one with the funky fish motif Noll kept from an old trip to Corsetti. Was that a blush on his face?

Cute. Noll almost chuckled. Then she didn't, because it would have been too strange to bridge the void of despair in her chest with such a cheerful sound. She glanced at the radar, a cruel habit now. The screen's emptiness complemented the one inside her.

What a stupid thing, forgetting for a moment why her world was breaking apart.

"How's Liepok?" she asked.

Temak's face emerged, the flush on it carefully eliminated. "Resting. Maybe sleeping. It's hard to tell with them."

"They're not taking this well."

"Their whole crew is gone. Everyone they know out here. No wonder."

No wonder at all. Noll took a long gulp of the coffee. The hot liquid burnt its way through her. "So, why'd *you* come here?"

Back in the muck of No Man's Land and then the chaos of the crossing, she had no time or capacity to wonder, but Temak didn't have much of a reason to follow her. And he'd never given an explanation.

He gave an easy shrug. "It felt like a bad enough idea."

Noll glared at him. Together with his previous statement, he really did sound like he thought her completely mad. Wouldn't be the first person, to be fair.

Then after a moment of silence, Temak added, "Let's say, I don't have the best experiences with the sort of...delaying the inevitable we might have expected if we stayed. Twiddling our thumbs, waiting for patrol and the lane scientists while our window was literally closing."

Noll raised an eyebrow. *Oh, intrigue.* "Why, what kind of experiences do you have?"

Temak sighed. "You weren't in the Foggy Cities when the Union attacked, were you?"

She shook her head and finished up her cup. It landed on the dashboard with a fine clang. "We live on Metallia."

"That place fared relatively well, didn't it?"

"More or less." She shrugged to dispel the uncomfortable push of bad memories. "During the riots on those Union planets, a small unit of destroyers appeared above Metallia City. Scared the hells out of us. A demonstration of power so that we didn't dare to try anything similar. There were random raids, skirmishes. A long curfew. Casualties. Not a lot, but...enough."

Cold, ghastly fingers closed around her throat. She didn't want to remember.

Metallia had been on the fringes of Union control: Leadership must have thought it was worth more to oversee the merchant world from the shadows rather than switching off its profitable mechanisms entirely. But when the riots had started, the Net organizing its disparate pieces to finally strike, Leadership was scrambling. It was doing everything it could to prove its supremacy and control the unrest, and things changed sharply from one day to the other. The Foggy Cities were a strategic center, the beating heart of lanehunter culture, and when they fell, everything had become fluid. All the bad outcomes were suddenly possible. Yes, the polite thing to say was that Metallia had avoided the brunt of it, but everyone who survived that week carried it with them now, forever.

The impotence. The terror. Every single one of Noll's nightmares coming true, manifesting her fear of not being able to save herself and the people she loved because someone else, something else way above her was deciding over her fate. And she was nothing in the crossfire, nothing at all.

"I'm sorry," Temak said. The way he looked at her, he understood, too. "The Cities got the brunt of the hellfire, and I don't know how much it could have been mitigated if we reacted better, but...we should have."

THROUGH A WINDOW DARKLY

Noll swallowed around the memory of her misery. "What happened?"

A bitter smile flashed through the man's face. "Cities-dwellers are not like nomadic lanehunters. Not like you. They tried to wait the siege out, hoping for a miracle, struggling to even process the possibility that their stronghold was breached. They played for time, bargained with fate. They thought themselves invincible, trusting it would be alright when they should have gone packing the moment the first enforcers set their dirty boots on Central's streets." Temak gulped down the last of his coffee. "Me and my friends, we tried to tell them. As lower-ranking Net members, we only had a little more understanding of what was going on, but we had that. We tried. We tried."

He stopped talking, his eyes averted, fixed on the screens. Noll decided not to ask about those friends. His story resonated with all the hidden parts of herself; Temak had gone through the exact same thing as her, from another angle.

"Everything we had was lost in mere hours," the man added, uttering the words slowly. "I was not in the right position to change things. One of these days, I plan to be."

Fuck, okay. "Still. Way to jump into the unknown with a rando."

Temak's mouth curled to a slight smile. "I had a good feeling about you. You seemed sure of yourself."

"I was," Noll grunted. "Past tense."

"You were right. Someone had to take to the frontlines. Not sure what people on Duplex-1 can see now...maybe their Window is gone, maybe the tunnel is broken up into several pieces, but even if they were organizing some neat and disciplined rescue mission, they clearly didn't make it through. They're way further from doing something worthwhile than us."

"We're too far as well." The radar screen flashed empty. The *Taro* was getting farther and farther away from the Window in its expanding bubble shell of search. Where was Jayce? Perhaps he wasn't even here.

Perhaps there'd been another exit before this one that they'd all missed, and now he was floating alone in another distant corner of the universe, helpless and scared to death. She suppressed the whimper trying to crawl its way up her throat. "Sometimes there's no hope of doing anything worthwhile. Sometimes you suffer whatever is dealt."

Temak shook his head. "Not as long as there's a way left. Not until blood is flowing in our veins and breath lives in our lungs."

Noll found her mouth pulling to a faint grin. The man sounded like a warrior, someone utterly devout. Foolish, of course. But it lit a small fire in her stomach.

"Thanks," she whispered.

They both glared at the instruments together for a while in silence. Anxiety and fear crept back in. Not counting down each of Jayce's remaining minutes of oxygen was the hardest thing Noll had ever tried to do. And what would she do if time was up, there was still blood in her veins and breath in her lungs, but she couldn't find him?

The thought was poison. She needed to distract herself. She needed to move, do something, anything. Even if it was just walking to the other room so Temak didn't see the tears gathering in her eyes.

"I'll be back," she said, pushing herself out of the seat. Temak lifted his warm brown eyes at her. "Don't touch anything. It's gonna alert me if it found something, okay?"

"No problem, captain," he replied. It looked like he wanted to say something else, too, but in the end, he nodded.

Noll nodded back gratefully. *Good talk. Good man.* She spun around to leave the cockpit as fast as was physically possible, and Temak went back to stare at the screens.

4

Temak's last words rang in Noll's ears as she swiped the tears out of her eyes and left him behind in the cockpit. Between her and Jayce, it didn't make sense talking about a captain—the two of them were the most crew the *Taro* had ever seen since they'd scavenged her together. Whenever, occasionally, they had problem figuring out whose plan to follow, they fought valiantly for the right to choose. Verbally. Mostly.

Noll wasn't a captain. She was a part of this ship. A cog, on her better days. But the *Taro's* cave-like interior felt alien without her twin now. It was just a place, and it never should have been just a place.

Liepok sat in one of the chairs at the table in the living compartment, staring into the air. *Clearly not sleeping, what in hells was Temak talking about?* As Noll plopped down in the other chair, the Nefirn followed her with their eyes. She imagined patient waiting in them, but she really had no idea what they were thinking.

And suddenly, no idea what to tell them either.

"Search is still on," she mumbled. "Nothing so far, but we'll keep at it."

Liepok made a humming sound. Their voice was thin, shaky. Noll wanted to ask, not for the first time, whether they thought there was a chance they'd find their crew alive, but she wasn't sure how to phrase it. *"Hey, so, do you expect they're still breathing out there somehow, or, you know, they're dead and coming after them into the big stinking nothing was some kind of strange expression of reverence? Just asking. Making light conversation."*

But the Nefirn didn't talk, and Noll was left scrambling for something to say again. "If you're hungry, I have some—"

"No, thank you. I'm fine now," they said, followed by a long exhale. "Better, at least."

Noll only grumbled something. Luckily, Liepok spoke again. "Thank you for bringing me here." The beginnings of a faint smile appeared on their face. Grateful.

"Of course." The air thinned in Noll's lungs. "I wasn't about to forbid you or anything."

Unexpectedly and for the first time they'd been stuck here, she thought about the Krotke twins' family. She didn't know their parents well, but they had loads of common friends. In a way, she was here in their places, too, wasn't she? To look for their sons. She wasn't only responsible for Jayce. Now that it occurred to her, at least.

Great. Didn't necessarily need this, thanks, brain.

"I barely know them, can you imagine? I only met them...uh, it was, um...five months ago, I think?" The openness of Liepok's statements jarred Noll out of her dark thoughts. The Nefirn's eyes unfocused as if they were thinking hard about something. Maybe converting their own timekeeping? "My kiahra...my nest, my family, is back home. On Meya. You know it as Nefirn-4."

Noll stayed silent. For some reason, she was afraid any interruption would stop Liepok from sharing more. But her face must have been empathetic enough because the Nefirn went on.

"Our captain, their name is Frahyss. I know them more than the others. They're very nice. Back home, they've done a lot for bringing the community together. Started all kinds of different ventures. They brought us all here so we could find our own way. I know the language because they taught me." Liepok swept a finger over the back of their hand hesitantly, the scales bristling. "This was our first chance to see the world."

Like a dark meteor eclipsing the sun, reality shadowed Liepok's gentle words. Their first chance, and it ended like this.

Noll grasped for something, anything that might provide a cheerier topic. "So, your planet is okay now? Your system? After the Union cleared out?"

THROUGH A WINDOW DARKLY

She didn't know a lot about Nefirns, probably even less than the average lanehunter off of Metallia. Their solar system had five habitable planets they'd settled on before humans had ever popped up around those parts, and they'd been among the first aliens subdued by the Union when its Leadership had started conquering the galaxy a couple hundred years ago. They were used as laborers, their planets mined and exploited for metals and other resources and under heavy lockdown. Until recently, few of their people ever left the system, and the occasional refugee spoke little about their worlds, their culture, and what they'd suffered.

Liepok's eyes glinted at her question—not necessarily like a human's would which was usually more of a synchronized product of parallel physical reactions: pupils dilating, the eyelids lifting, the head rearing up lightly, or the mouth pulling to a faint smile. This really *was* a glint like something physically happened inside the Nefirn's pupils. It made Noll conscious of how little she knew about Nefirn biology as well.

And conscious of how infrequently she worked with aliens, in general. Huge oversight, honestly.

"Things are much better," Liepok said. "We can finally govern ourselves. We're finally free. We've forgotten what it is like, so it's hard. Look at me!" The strange little heaving sound coming through their air converter could barely be called a laugh. "I have no idea what I'm doing. But I'm proud of ourselves. That this happened in my generation, even with outside help. We stood up to the Union. We lost much, but now all of us can do our part and find our place again."

The monologue flooded out of them in one breath like they were waiting for the occasion to tell this to someone the whole time. Noll smiled, despite herself. "Sounds neat. And what would you do out here? What's your place?"

"Oh, I have no idea yet," they replied. Something was happening to the scales around their neck and face, the color changing from faint blue to iridescent pink and gentle yellow. Their face still barely showed emotion, but Noll began to understand Nefirns didn't express themselves like that at all. And of course, they weren't, but seeing it was different than knowing. Suddenly, she was curious whether whenever Liepok smiled or frowned, it was for the sake of humans around them, and in what other ways they'd share their emotions with their own people. "I don't even know what options I have," Liepok went on. "I need to see things and places, know how others live. Humans. The other spacefaring races. And my people, the ones who got out earlier. That was the goal. But Captain Frahyss wants to be like you. A lanehunter."

"Hah! Good luck to that!" Noll couldn't help but snort. But it sounded too sharp, too rude, so she dulled her next words. The cold facts about what Captain Frahyss could or couldn't choose as their profession in the current situation lay in ambush on the grim borderlands of this conversation anyway. There was no reason to add to that darkness. "No, I'm serious. I always say, if you don't find yourself an attractive planet you're satisfied with, the best you can do is to go out there and claim everything. Why not? The universe is huge and more attainable than ever."

"But dangerous," Liepok added. Their voice was careful again. "Right? You need to know how to protect yourself."

Noll waved it away. "You need to know that everywhere."

"Not back at home. We never had the option of protecting ourselves. We didn't have the need, because we didn't have control. We forgot how to be free, how to organize ourselves, invent things. They've been trying to break us for too long." The Nefirn halted for a second, something heavy leaving its imprint on their posture. But they went on, their shoulders twisting in discomfort. "I don't like to think of ourselves like that, but it's true. We want to act against it, and that's good. Our wish for adventure is not dead yet. Many took off like we did, and many stayed behind to rebuild on the ruins. Reform what has been shaped wrongly."

They fell silent. It was as if Noll finally glimpsed Liepok in full daylight. She couldn't even imagine the situation they were coming from. The Union had truly fucked everyone in this rotten universe, hadn't they?

But the Nefirns were still here, trying to skip and step over the debris of the past carefully. Over that learned fear towards curiosity, towards bravery. Liepok had come after their crew even when there was barely any hope to begin with. Noll wanted to ask about the spacesuits again, but the promise of the answer was too terrible.

"I have to admit, it is chaotic out here," Liepok spoke again quietly. "It's too much, sometimes. How are you not always afraid?"

The question echoed inside Noll, bouncing between the walls of her diminishing self-control. After the conversation she'd had with Temak—how could she encourage Liepok?

"Of course, I'm afraid." Nothing but the truth could come out now. Liepok had that effect on her. Anyone else had asked, she'd have feigned. "Right now, even more. Without Jayce."

Liepok nodded. They did it so categorically, so methodically, that Noll was sure they made the gesture for her sake. How foreign this all must be for them! They needed to change even their basic behaviors to be understood out here. Maybe when seeing crowds of Nefirns outside of their system became an everyday occurrence, they could truly be themselves, without any pretending.

Frahyss, Liepok, and their big ship were just the beginning. A thread of hope to hold onto.

"You know, everyone talks about lanehunters as if we're these lone wolves, conquering lanes and ancient ruins by ourselves." She hadn't been planning on elaborating, but here she was. "It's bullshit. Almost all of us have some crew and not just to stare at the instruments or fix the burnt-out connections in the life-support system. Clans are the basic unit of our society for a reason. They formed from families. That means something." She shrugged. "Something sappy and world-defining, probably. But at least you're never really alone. You can't be."

Noll knew she was filtering the words through her own fright and loneliness. Voicing hopes she prayed every night were true. Oh, lanehunters loved to say they were self-sufficient, doing it for the number one, strictly for the profit. For many of them, it was true. Everyone sure fucking hated those guys' guts, too.

The only thing that ever comforted Noll when having to stare the beast of chaos in the eyes was that she wasn't staring by herself. Together with Jayce, yes, and maybe with others who had similar fears. Who'd, maybe, catch her when she fell.

The theory remained unproven. But always sowing seeds in her mind. Hope was awful like that.

Liepok smiled like they understood, and they seemed to like the thought. *Stars, now I* really *hope I'm not lying to this poor bastard.*

"That sounds nice," they said simply.

Noll nodded. "It helps, sometimes. Not always."

She glanced at her tablet, but there was no alert from the main computer. Jayce had so little oxygen left. Her stomach turned. The way she was sitting here, spouting nonsense about hope and community under the circumstances was...surreal.

The two of them sat in silence—one of mutual agreement, less awkward now. Minutes ticked by. Half-coherent, fear-shot thoughts whirled in Noll's head. For all she tried, she was panicking again.

Then the ship dipped around them, the room plummeting and correcting itself like the *Taro* had done a sharp evading maneuver where the artificial gravity grid couldn't compensate for it quick enough. Noll was familiar with the effect and managed to brace herself, but Liepok was so surprised they nearly fell out of their firmly fixed-to-the-deck chair.

THROUGH A WINDOW DARKLY

Noll grabbed their arm with a steadying hand but heard her tablet beep the exact same time. Her heart jumped to her throat. Something changed. They'd found something.

"You alright?" she asked. Liepok settled back in the chair, holding on for dear life, and nodded fervently. Noll jumped up. "Don't move, I'm gonna go and—"

She couldn't finish the sentence. A dull bang resounded from the tail, and the ship teetered again, lightly shaking.

Wait—is that? Was someone firing at them?!

Noll scooped up her tablet but only threw it a cursory look—status reports of the ship flooded the screen, according to which an explosive blow had just occurred against the shields at the *Taro's* tail section. She flew out of the living compartment back to the cockpit, stumbling over her own feet. In the corner of her eyes, she saw Liepok follow.

Temak sat in her pilot seat, typing something into the computer as the two of them crowded into the cabin. The ship veered to the side from the new trajectory changes.

"What's going on?" Noll pushed beside Temak, leaning over him in barely concealed allusion that she'd like to take over the piloting, thank you very much, but the man didn't react. He didn't even look at her. She raised her voice. "Who's shooting at us?"

A glance at the radar screen confirmed a single mark ahead of the *Taro*, and behind it, the Window's strong signal glinted in the distance. They'd turned around; Temak had interrupted their search to confront this new ship.

He still didn't react. Noll repeated her question even louder, and it finally made him register her presence. His forehead glistened with sweat, his eyes scanning her face nervously. Before he could have answered, another crash shook the ship.

Red alarms flashed on the dashboard. Their shields were still up, but if the hits kept coming, that might change soon.

"They came out of the Window," Temak mumbled. His fingers lay frozen on the keyboard, and the settings for the proton cannon filled the screen in front of him. "That's a Union nailship, Noll."

All the blood drained from Noll's limbs. Stars danced at the peripheries of her vision. It was the Union. And of course, it was. She should have known. Just another one of their cruel games to ruin everything.

"Get out of that chair," she hissed at Temak, the urge to *do something* flaring up with unyielding intensity. But all of his attention was on the instruments again as he smashed a button and launched another series of projectiles towards the nailship. Noll grasped his shoulder. "I said get out of the chair, Temak, or—"

Fire in her belly. Cold fear snaking around her throat. Her hand swung towards the gun in her holster, but she stopped herself. *Stars.*

The nailship's evasive maneuvers left a twirling spiral line on the radar screen, but the vessel was still heading towards the *Taro*, fast. Noll's mind turned, painfully slow. Did the Window lead to Union territory now? Did they have Jayce? Why were they sending a single nailship after them? What was happening on Duplex? Maybe whatever they were experiencing here was just the shadow of the real fight going on back there—

"Tell me what happened, please," she pleaded to Temak again. "It came out of the Window and shot at us?"

She glanced at Liepok who stood on Temak's other side. All their scales were ruffled up like fur on a scared cat.

"No," Temak grunted finally. "It came out of the Window, and *I* shot at it."

His face was not his own; it was a mask, a darkness behind his eyes Noll didn't want to look at. The same bitter emptiness she saw on him when he'd been talking about the attacks on the Foggy Cities.

He noticed her stunned silence. "It's a fucking nailship, Noll, what was I supposed to do? I'm sure they just want to talk."

THROUGH A WINDOW DARKLY

As if on cue, the comms released a trill signaling an incoming transmission. Without even thinking about it, Noll reached out to accept it.

Temak jumped so fast it was hard to follow, and he pushed Noll away from the dashboard. She collided with Liepok; the Nefirn lost balance and landed on the deck in an ugly flop, and before Noll could brace herself and turn at him, Temak had his gun out, pointed at her chest.

Noll froze. Her vision narrowed to the shaking hands of the man in front of her. He could off her in half a second, easily.

Man, I haven't been threatened with a gun in a while. Takes me the fuck back.

"We're not talking to them," Temak said, the words quick, slurred. "They'll say anything to trick us. Think a little. You know this. You know it as much as I do."

Noll couldn't see the screen, but there were no more collisions from enemy fire, and the comms were still indicating the incoming hail.

She steadied herself and took a step forward, heart in her throat, her ears buzzing. "Temak, you're dooming us all. Think about why we're here. We can try to take on them, but what if we don't have to?" Temak's hands were shaking. He was panicking. "What if...what if they have Jayce?"

Or what if the nailship was in a similar situation to them? As much as she hated to admit, things were not as simple as they'd been a few months ago. Encountering a nailship or Union agents didn't automatically mean shoot to kill anymore. Her fingers clenched into fists. If the ex-agent from Duplex Saori had said was there to "start a new life with a clean slate" was on that nailship, would she have blown her to smithereens? Jayce was dying somewhere out there, and Noll would just kill someone like that?

Why would they hail them if they'd come here to kill them?

"Noll, don't do it." Liepok clambered up behind her. Noll threw them a look of warning—the last thing they needed was a sudden move to spook Temak. But the Nefirn fixed their eyes on the Net spy. They held their arm, the coloration on their face white. "Temak, at least we should listen to them. Please..."

For fuck's sake. Noll cringed. If even this Nefirn, their planet and life nearly destroyed by the Union, would want to resort to a peaceful option, what did it say about her that she wanted to decide this with another series of proton cannon strikes right about now?

Because Temak was right. It *could* be a trick. Typical agent mind games. Not to mention they loved to board ships, question and torture their prey. Temak might be a wee bit traumatized, but he knew his stuff. He knew their methods, and Noll knew them, too. How many times had a nailship disguised itself as a broken-down vessel in trouble, and then swooped down on lanehunters when they let their guard down? How many times had agents attempted to raid the *Taro* at lane entries and exits, in the middle of nothing, over abandoned-looking ruins on dead worlds? They were a pest. Relentless. Once they got the upper hand, they showed no mercy.

They couldn't trust this. Who else had the technology to do something like this to the Window? The Talalans, maybe, but they weren't the ones prancing around over here, focusing serious firepower on them.

But if they had Jayce...

"You're not going to shoot me, Temak," Noll said, taking another step towards him. He wouldn't, right? *Come on, handsome. Don't tell me I was wrong about you.* "I know you're not. Let's do this together, okay?"

He didn't move. The call from the nailship was still going off. Temak had quickly toppled over to the far side of rational thinking, but honestly, Noll couldn't blame him. Not even for shooting first.

THROUGH A WINDOW DARKLY

But the seconds ticked by. If they couldn't get to an agreement, they were all lost. And Jayce was lost, too.

5

Right. Fuck this.

Noll dropped her shoulders and straightened her back. "Everyone take a deep breath and calm down, okay?" She even showed what she meant with a big inhale and exhale.

But no one reacted. The *Taro* was shaking; the comms were still blaring; Temak was still pretending he'd shoot her. Noll put her hands on her hips and went on impatiently. "But, you know, hurry the fuck up, because we've got stuff to do."

Temak blinked as if waking from a bad dream. "Do you have a plan?"

Plan? Noll had never been more at her wits end. "Listening to this thing called brain in my skull, first of all," she said quickly. "Not my strongest organ, that honoured title has to go to my kidneys, but you gotta give it to the little buddy, it's trying. Listen, of course, we can't trust this. I bet they cooked up this whole mess. But we can't explode them out of the sky. I repeat: what if they have our people?" She glanced at Liepok. The Nefirn stood flattened against the inner hull—they hadn't moved since Temak's outburst. "I don't want to be at their mercy, but we need information. And for that, we need to hurt them first. Hit their weak points, make sure they have to rely on us."

Temak shook his head. "It's not gonna be easy."

Noll's eyes darkened. "Duh. That's why I suggest you do your job, Mr Spyface, instead of waving your gun around. There are other ways to shut me up. Leave the bad ideas to me for now?"

She held out a hand, asking for his gun, although she was pretty sure he'd never give it to her. But the expression of tense panic on Temak's face softened, the muzzle of his plasma pistol wavering. *There you go. Don't force me to knock you out.* If she even could. Dude was a sort of soldier, after all.

The man relaxed his arms. Then finally, dropped them beside his body. His lips trembled as he looked at Noll, eyes clearing. "Fuck. I'm— I didn't want to— shit." He glanced at Liepok. "I shouldn't have reacted like that."

"I still think we should talk to them," Liepok muttered. "We shot first."

And we're about to, again. "I'm sorry, Li, but we don't know the game they're playing." Noll threw a cautious look at Temak. She wanted to trust him, but he *had* pulled a gun on her. "We need an advantage first."

"But they won't tell us anything if we keep fighting them." The Nefirn's voice was barely audible.

The comms decided this was the perfect moment to fall silent. Whatever the nailship had wanted, they'd given up on it.

Noll waited for the bone-chilling, nauseating feeling that the thought of any kind of negotiation with the Union had woken in her to subside, but it didn't. There was only regret. That ship had sailed. But when Temak threw her a questioning look, it pulled her back into the moment. She nodded at him, and the man lunged for the pilot chair without a word, taking control of the *Taro* once again.

It was up to him now. Noll was a decent pilot and shot, but as a Net operative, Temak had to know nailships and their weaknesses even better than her. She simply would have run a scan and risked another series of shots towards where she suspected the engine and weapon controls on the enemy vessel, but if they wanted to disable it without destroying it, they needed higher precision.

She prayed to the sky full of stars Temak had the skills. And that there wouldn't be a swarm of other nailships coming after this one through the Window in two minutes.

THROUGH A WINDOW DARKLY

"Li." She turned the Nefirn. "Sit down, okay? This is gonna be bumpy."

She pointed at the co-pilot seat, and Liepok obeyed, although Noll could practically feel the disapproval radiating off them. Temak squinted at the Nefirn as they strapped themself in. Shame was an open wound on his face, but he didn't say anything.

He turned the *Taro* around, circling to face the nailship once again. The enemy vessel's trajectory changes were erratic like it was expecting their next barrage, but it was only firing intermittently now. Maybe they already had problems with maneuvring. Maybe this would be fine. Noll grasped the back of Liepok's seat, and then everything happened really fast.

Temak opened fire, targeting three well-defined points on the nailship's hull—weapon systems or shield core, Noll suspected. The vessel fired back, making the *Taro* veer to the side to avoid it—a blast exploded against their shield, but judging from the strength of the jolt, it was mostly absorbed. And Temak was not giving up. He zoomed past the Union ship and spun around in a vertical loop so sharply the artificial grav went wobbly again, and Noll lost her footing for a couple of seconds. Liepok's hand shot out and held onto her wrist in a strange echo of how Noll had done the same for them before.

In a fraction of a second, Temak stabilized them and got the nailship into his crossfire again. Explosions bloomed on the screen, the *Taro* barely evading the scattering debris. As they left it behind again, the nailship looked like a heap of garbage on the radar screen.

"I think I did it," Temak said, his jaw tensing. "I think—"

A rumble cut him off as the *Taro* jolted forward like something had collided with it from the back. Alerts screeched—generator, hull stability, oxygen supply. Noll yelled out a desparate sound without words as if she could get the situation under control with the power of her voice, and then—

Something exploded. A force pushed Noll across the dashboard and crashing against the screens, but before she could feel the collision, all went dark and the world ceased to exist.

Everything hurt. It was cold. It was dark. Silence rang dead in her ears, and stars, everything *hurt*.

Noll opened her eyes and realized she'd been wrong. For example, her head definitely hadn't hurt until then. But now that she was staring into the *Taro's* sharp red emergency lights, pain like all hells sprung up at the nape of her neck, driving a weak whine out of her mouth.

She lay sprawled under the dashboard, and for some reason, there was a helmet on her head, her right cheek flattened against its cool plastic, her breaths echoing dully in the narrow space. It wasn't the compact thing—just the one part of their normal space suits, usually stored outside by the airlock. The body part itself was missing, so she was still wearing her frayed cargo pants and red jacket. Twisting her neck, she found an O_2-canister plopped onto the floor beside her.

She scanned the cockpit and tried to focus her blurry vision. A single figure wearing a silvery suit and helmet stood beside the closed entrance hatch with their back at her.

Heart jumping into her throat, she tried to remember what in hells she'd been doing when someone apparently decided to drive her over with a tank. Memories drifted, scattered in her brain. The Window. Jayce. The conversation with Liepok. Temak's revolt. They'd wanted to disable the nailship, and it had been going promising, until—

She must have moved or made a noise because the strange figure turned to her. Noll couldn't see their face, not even the eyes behind

THROUGH A WINDOW DARKLY

the gleaming visor. "Don't you even try," they said through her helmet comms. "Stay where you are."

The voice sounded familiar, but Noll couldn't place it. Her thoughts were foggy, and thinking harder wasn't bringing more results, so she attempted to gather her limbs and stand up.

"I said do not move!" the figure snapped. Their hand moved towards something on their belt, and it made Noll plop back onto her backside. "I'd love to shoot you and honestly, there's not much that's holding me back right now, so think carefully before you act!"

Damn, why was their voice so familiar? The answer floated out of her reach as the red light burned tears out of her eyes. She couldn't focus. There was a ticking in her mind that became louder and louder.

Time. Yes. There was no time. Jayce had no time left.

The figure turned back to the switchboard opening on the wall beside the hatch. Noll desperately tried to gather the pieces of the scene in some semblance of an ordered pile. Red lights. Emergency lights. Auxiliary power? Okay, the *Taro* was on auxiliary power. There was a helmet on her head and a whole-ass suit on the person who had yelled at her, so, no oxygen in here. Perhaps the ship had gotten breached. But pressure was fine, and the cockpit seemed secure. The engine wasn't on, though, judging from the lack of the subtle tremble under her palm when she placed it on the deck.

Her pulse climbed another notch. Liepok and Temak. What had happened to them?

She flopped her body around awkwardly, pain shooting up her limbs. Someone was lying on the deck not far from her, but...it was hard to say exactly what she was seeing. The person had a helmet on as well, and they weren't wearing the suit part either. Instead, their body below the neck was wrapped in a strange, half-translucent material. Organic-looking like a thick flap of skin or pale, sturdy, naked wings. Noll pulled herself closer, reached out carefully to touch. The material was cold and rigid but gave a little like flexible membrane. Its bluish-grey hue was broken up by darker blue veins…but what—

Liepok?

Their clothes were difficult to see under the skin…thing, but the closed pair of eyes through the visor could have been them, and the skinny, lean body sure looked more like the Nefirn than Temak. They didn't stir at Noll's scrutiny, but the faint rise and fall of their chest indicated they were alive.

Noll glanced around again, careful not to draw the attention of the silvery-suited stranger. There was a heap of clothes lying on the deck farther away. Could be another body. Temak?

Before she could have crawled up to them, someone pushed the cockpit hatch open, its clank a dull sound through her helmet. As the newcomer hurried in and sealed the cockpit again, Noll's hands moved towards the gun on her belt. Promptly finding the holster empty.

Fair. That was expected. The agents had taken her blaster.

Because they had to be the agents, didn't they?

"Life support should work now," the second figure said, their voice hollow in the helmet radio. Same suit, same helmet as the other. Not something Noll ever saw Union goons wear, but the tech seemed to be up there. "You can turn it back on."

The other one fiddled with the switchboard again. This, Noll at least understood. They'd done something similar once before with Jayce when a landing had gone badly and knocked out the generator. They had to reroute what little their emergency batteries could sustain—oxygen, life support, electricity—to the cockpit while they whomped the generator back into shape. Even artificial gravity had to be turned off in the tail section for a while.

So when the red lights blinked out, giving way to the Taro's normal illumination, a low, healthy buzz filled the room, and gentle airflow touched her skin, Noll wasn't surprised. She also discovered she could move her arm now.

THROUGH A WINDOW DARKLY

"Li?" she hissed, shaking the prone body beside her lightly. "Li, can you hear me? Are you okay?"

For a few seconds, there was no reaction. Then the skin thing around their body twitched and started...contracting? Noll stared at it, trying to figure it out, but in the span of a couple of moments, whatever it had been, the thing was gone, revealing Liepok's body and drab clothes under it. A few moments later, the Nefirn opened their eyes behind the helmet visor and rolled over, freeing their arms from under them.

"I'm alive," they croaked. "I'm alive. Are you okay?" Their head snapped towards the heap of clothes to the side. "And Temak—"

"What did I *just* tell you about moving around?" The figure at the switchboard stalked closer to Noll. She thought they were going to grab her or something, but they stopped in front of her as if colliding with a wall, as if thinking better of it. They gaped at her—although their eyes still weren't visible—for a long moment.

A shiver ran through Noll. There was something wrong about the person's movements, about how they spoke to her. And as the stranger towered above her, suddenly it felt more important than anything for them not to take another step towards her, not to utter another word.

No such luck. Before Noll could obey her sudden revulsion and back off, the agent reached for their helmet and unclasped it from around their neck with a quick motion.

And then, Noll was staring into her own face.

What the—

Her face. Her eyes. *Her* lips pressed into a thin line, *her* eyebrows flattened into a frown that was barely there.

What in the world is going on here?

For a long moment, no one moved. Noll clicked the helmet off her head. Stars danced in front of her eyes; she needed to breathe freely. The *other* didn't stop her as she climbed onto her feet and scooted back against the consoles as far as she could. Liepok followed her example, getting rid of their head gear. Noll could feel them trembling beside her.

This isn't normal. This really isn't normal. Am I dreaming?

The other agent, the one with their head still covered, sighed, their whole body collapsing inward from the movement. "Alright. Back off, both of you." They pulled off their helmet, too, and the world turned with Noll again. It was the ex-agent chick they'd left behind on Duplex.

"Y-you?" she stuttered. "How?"

She felt the last strings of her sanity escape her grasp. She held her whirling head. *Focus, idiot. Focus, focus, focus.*

"Parallel realities," the agent muttered. Her eyes were wide as she took a step closer to *her* Noll, placing what felt like a soothing hand on her shoulder. Both of them seemed much less sure of what to do than a moment before.

Noll's mind pushed against it. No, they were lying. They must have given her, all of them, something. A drug, some hallucinogen, that was why she was confused. Or maybe they cloned her, somehow? Agents were clones, right?

But when? Why her and why now? What was the con? What had they done to Jayce?

She realized it was the only question that mattered.

She stood up as straight as she could, pushing down the disgust waking in her when she looked into the eyes of her doppelganger. "You have my brother, don't you? What do you want from us?"

The other her sighed. Noll cringed, although she tried to expect it. That was her sigh. Her voice. Stars, she was going mad.

"We don't have him," her double said. "I have no idea what's going on. Wallace did say he saw strange space-time dilution signals through the Window, so...this must be it, I guess."

"Wallace?" Noll's brain grabbed on the first thing she could process. "You know Wallace?"

THROUGH A WINDOW DARKLY

"Yes," the second agent said, measured. "And if you know him too, and you're looking for your brother, then…"

"Then we're here for the same thing," the other Noll finished shakily. "I'm looking for him, too."

The ticking in Noll's head returned, stronger than ever. They didn't have him. They didn't have Jayce. And so then… She glanced at the dashboard clock, and her heart plummeted.

Very best case scenario, Jayce had fifteen minutes of oxygen left.

Somehow, she kept herself on her wobbling legs. "Have you found any trace of him?"

"Before or after you shot us out of the sky?"

Fucking hells.

This was impossible. Had these two really come from some parallel reality? No one had ever found a lane leading out of the universe. There was talk, sure—there was always talk. Lanes and cracks to the past or the future, to worlds similar but eerily different to theirs. No one ever proved it. Even crossing lanes to other galaxies was exceedingly rare and highly, *highly* dangerous.

No time travel. No multiverse. If they existed, they were unavailable.

Noll's glance shifted to the unmoving body of Temak. He would know what questions to ask to get to the truth.

"He doesn't have enough oxygen," she muttered. She locked eyes with the other Noll. "He's out there somewhere, and he's going to suffocate in a few minutes."

Noll-2's impossible gaze fixed on her, an expression that seemed to hold something else at bay on her face. "Yeah."

Like staring into a twisted mirror. The other her's hair was different, and the lines on her face had been formed by different experiences, but her being, her core was the same. She felt it. That intangible thing, comprising of all the subtle exterior and interior characteristics and at the same time being more and less than those—it shone in both of them. Same sides of the magnet.

Maybe that was why she repulsed her. It was all wrong.

"You have to roll with it."

Her twin's voice echoed in her head through the unknown vasts of space and time. He had been sitting with her at a rickety aluminum table, counting the meager pile of doubloons in front of him with pretend care while clanking music blasted from a machine in the corner. It was somewhat after midnight in one of the mustiest bars of Metallia City. They'd gone broke again.

"You have to roll with it or it will roll over you." Jayce flashed his teeth in a proud smile as if he'd just won jackpot when the exact opposite was the case. Noll's chest clenched in warm affection as he went on. *"And you can only go where you see the road, so never close your eyes, okay?"*

Noll blinked away the vision, breathed out. "Okay. Let's say the same thing happened to you guys as to us. Window got all funky, people were pulled through, you followed in to save them." The agents nodded firmly to each statement. Neither of them were grappling for their guns for now. It was somewhere to start. "Who? Who were pulled through?"

"The Krotke twins," Noll-2 answered quietly. "Some bystanders, Nefirns, I think." She glanced at Liepok. "I know you. From The Candle."

Liepok bristled but didn't speak. "Well, I know *you*," Noll said instead, addressing the agent from Duplex. "You wanted to come through with us, but I didn't trust you because you're an agent. Are you...her?"

She looked roughly the same, but then again, it wasn't like she'd ever studied her closely. Could she expect an honest answer? Could she trust anything these two said?

THROUGH A WINDOW DARKLY

A shadow passed over the woman's face. "I'm... I'm Mai. I don't think I'm her, I already—" She glanced at her Noll again. "We've been together since forever. All three of us came from the Union when it fell. In our...world. Recently. We're not the bad guys."

Noll-2 gave a snort, and Noll caught her eyes flit at Temak. "We didn't shoot first, at least. He's gonna be fine, by the way. Messed himself up good when you lost pressure for a sec there. You two were protected by the veil shell." She nodded at Liepok. "Good thing we got here in time to patch the hole up and help out with the helmets."

Well, some of that made sense. While Noll attempted to process, Noll-2 went to crouch beside Temak's prostate form and finally removed his helmet with a greater care than was expected judging from her crude tone before.

Noll crept closer to see. The man's face was colorless, eyes sunken, skin clammy. He was taking shallow breaths, but he was unconscious.

Liepok stared at him like Temak was already dead. What had Noll-2 just said? Noll had been protected by what? A veil shell? Was that the thing around Liepok before?

"This was not how we wanted this to go," Liepok said, speaking for the first time during the conversation. Their body trembled as they glanced at Mai and the other Noll. "I'm sorry. We're sorry. It's obvious we have to work together. Right?"

Their voice was surprisingly calm, friendly. *No, not calm*, Noll realized. Resigned.

The other Noll just stared at them. What was she thinking? When she'd said she was looking for her brother too, Noll believed her. She was an agent, she was *her*, but somehow, she was here for the same thing.

Noll could use that.

"They're right. All of us want the same thing," Mai said as if she read her thoughts. "To find those we lost. But our ship is broken, and yours needs some serious intervention. We still have a chance, but we need to work together. Can you do that?"

She was talking to Noll—both Nolls, judging by her eyes flitting between them. And although every single cell of hers was fighting against working with her twisted mirror version, Noll knew the answer was obvious.

"Why do you think we have a chance?" she asked. Fifteen minutes. *Fifteen.*

Mai and Noll-2 communicated with stares and frowns for a few seconds, and Noll watched their silent chat, impatient. Finally, Mai sighed. "Going by all we can safely assume, we are indeed dealing with...parallel universes. And this must be a third one, different than the ones either of us belong to. Wallace thought the signal came from here—whatever someone did to change the Window. As we came through, we scanned the environment, and although we didn't find...uh, bodies, we did catch something. A moon or a station, too weak to locate. And then you exploded us, so we didn't have time to get more data."

"We didn't see anything, and we've been searching for hours," Noll muttered. Agents and their tech. More sensitive scanners, of course. No wonder they'd detected something the *Taro* couldn't.

Mai made a face. "Unfortunately, I don't have the numbers memorized. It wasn't this far out, for sure. The computer might have the data, but like I said, the ship is dead. I'd need time and help to resusitate the system."

"There was something else," Noll-2 said. She nodded towards the sky dense with distant stars through one of the screens. "Something at the borders of this solar system we couldn't identify. A sort of radiation."

"We saw that," Noll said. The mention of it made her shiver all over again.

"Did you also notice it was approaching?"

THROUGH A WINDOW DARKLY

The what?

"Very slowly," Mai added. "It will take years, but the signal was definitely moving in. From all directions."

There was a beat of silence from all of them.

"This place is *weird* weird," Noll-2 concluded.

Noll couldn't argue. Everything was upside down, topsy-turvy. And none of it could bring Jayce back to her. Not in fifteen minutes.

She looked at Noll-2, fearful. And as if the panic in the other's eyes reached out and grabbed her by the heart, instead of disgust, all she felt now was connection.

They were the same. They were thinking the same thing. The same push was there, in both of them. If she needed to trust something, she'd trust this.

If this mess had been planned and not by the Union, then someone had stolen people, friends and family, from two universes. It certainly didn't feel like a coincidence or a fatal accident. There was a meaning to it. There had to be. Stars, there had to be.

There were a lot of horrible things in this universe happening without any sense. This couldn't be one of them.

"So, what do we do?" Liepok asked the question.

Fifteen minutes. Both going back to the nailship to get the signal coordinates and starting up the *Taro* to journey to the edge of the solar system would have taken more time than fifteen minutes. Which meant if there was no plan, no intention behind what had happened, Jayce was already dead.

She turned the thought in her mind like dry, dusty stones. Denial was not something her twin ever condoned, but it was useful now. They had to start somewhere, and she was going to find where.

Even if she had to break the stupid multiverse apart to do it.

6

"Everything is connected." Noll forced her voice under a blanket of calm. "We need to figure out how. This place, this version of the Window—there has to be more to it. Whatever weirdness is at the edge of this system might tell us more."

The other option would be to waste time here praying the nailship back to life and cajole the data they needed out of its broken systems. Then search for a needle in a smorgasbord of broken-up asteroid matter—that was, a mysterious moon in the middle of nothing. The thought of leaving her scans unfinished—giving up on the only thing she'd been able to accomplish—physically hurt her, but the search was, at this point, hopeless. At least with a new plan, they would be moving towards a solid goal. Doing something.

But her pretend determination didn't seem to impress the two agents. They glanced at each other, frowns deepening, and then Mai stepped up to Noll-2 to draw her aside, talking to her in a low voice.

Noll's head ached from panic. She bounced on her heels, trying to think through the ticking in her head. *I know. I know. I'm trying, Jayce.*

She looked at Liepok. "What do you think?"

The Nefirn shifted their eyes from the two agents, clasped their fingers in front of their chest, and slow-blinked at Noll. With a human, it could have indicated worry, exhaustion. "I don't know," they muttered. "I'm going wherever you say to go."

"Li, no. I'm serious. My brother..." Her heart was beating in her throat, and the air was thin in her lungs, but she said it anyway. She had to say it. "I'm not sure he's still alive. But your people...if you think they might be—"

She stopped because Liepok's small smile was so sad her heart trembled in it. The Nefirn took a big breath before speaking, the air converter faintly buzzing in their throat. "My people ran out of time a long time ago. We can't last for long in the veil shell."

Noll's jaw tightened. *Shit.* Had Liepok known this back when they'd had that conversation in the living compartment? They never mentioned it.

"Veil shell? Is that the thing you had around you when—" Noll stopped again. The Nefirn's entire body went through such a transformation in a snap second. The smile disappeared, their scales and skin whitened, and even their hair seemed to stand straight up on their head.

But it only lasted for a moment, gone before Noll could ask whether they were okay. Liepok slow-blinked again, drawing back from her almost imperceptibly. "It's hard to explain. Not a lot of people know, but...it's a part of us. Defense mechanism, ceremonial attire, and more. It's a...uh, private thing."

Their eyes shifted to the deck. Noll felt herself go red. *Oh. Oh. Okay. Alright.*

"Well, thank you," she said. Liepok had saved her life. With this personal, perhaps even forbidden-to-show part of themself. She glanced up and saw Noll-2 and Mai drift apart, so she reached out for Liepok, not touching only hovering her fingers above their shoulder. "Seriously. Thank you. I'm...sorry for your group. We're going to figure this out, I promise."

Liepok nodded and gave another faint smile.

Mai stepped up to her. "Okay, are we doing this or what?" It seemed like the two of them had made their decision. Mai seemed more collected and calmer than before, but Noll-2 avoided everyone's eyes. Her face was grey, and she leaned to the console as if she could collapse at any minute.

Noll herself probably looked exactly the same. "Yep," she said. She planted her hands on her hips. Gotta project confidence. "We'll fix up the generator, check the engines, and head out to the edge of the solar system. While we work, we can continue to scan—maybe that moon or whatever pops up this time."

There was only a slight hesitation in Mai's affirmative nod. "Let's get to it."

She looked at Noll expectantly, and for a moment, she didn't know what to do. Sure, she'd rather go with Mai than with doppelganger-from-the-bottom-of-hells, but then Liepok would have been left alone here with *her*, and—

Damn. What did it say about her that she trusted Big Bad Agent Mai more than her own other self right now?

"Go," Liepok said, reading her thoughts. "We'll make ourselves useful in the meantime."

Mai was already moving, picking up and handing Noll her helmet on the way to the hatch. Noll wasn't sure where the suit part had gone, but if pressure was okay in the ship, they probably wouldn't need it. And the hull should be fine, right?

She *really* hoped it was fine. Jayce would be livid, otherwise.

Noll-2 leaned over the dashboard, running her eyes over the few instruments which were online on reserve power, and—Noll felt like—pointedly avoiding her eyes. So, she just waved at Liepok in what she hoped was an encouraging gesture. Stars, when did she become so protective of them? But they'd protected her, too. It was natural.

She walked up to a storage cabinet and pried a small toolbox out of it. If this wasn't enough to fix whatever was wrong with the ship, they were in trouble.

When she turned back, Noll-2 was sitting in her pilot chair.

The sight had an immediate effect on her. Blood boiling, breath hitched, she took a step forward, only to be stopped by a small cough. Liepok, now crouching beside Temak and fiddling with something that looked like an ultra-modern version of a medpack, glared at her with caution in their eyes. Noll could almost hear them trying to convince her telepathically to not freak out.

She tried. She tried hard, and in the end, succeeded. Liepok was right. They needed to work together.

Mai, now in helmet, called out to her, so she at least had something to distract herself with. The two of them slipped out to the hallway and quickly shut the door behind them. There might be fumes. Circulation needed to be checked first.

They stalked through the hallways, the living compartment, the cargo hold, and past the airlocks, then climbed down to the service hallway. Inspecting the inner hull as they went, everything seemed intact by eye and diagnostics—what breach there had been, a head-sized hole directly beside the airlock, the two agents had plugged in with a high-tech slime-looking substance when they'd arrived. It would last, Mai noted laconically. The hole had caused their O_2-levels to drop—which consequently knocked Temak out while Liepok could protect themself and Noll from more serious deprivation for a few minutes.

In any case, hull integrity was okay now and oxygen has been replenished from the emergency stores. That allowed them to leave the helmets behind as Noll scrolled through the status reports on her tablet and paired the warnings with real-life smoking, sparking, or darkened hubs and cables in the walls. The more serious ones she quick-fixed immediately, replacing the more important connections or switches. The nailship must have pumped a couple of huge plasma balls into the *Taro*—that was what usually zapped the systems like this. Although this one had fired with a larger flux, more characteristic of what a destroyer would do. A potential difference between their world and Noll's.

She still had trouble comprehending that. Parallel worlds. It felt so absurd.

Ever so often she instructed Mai to hand her something or check a display on the other side of the hallway, but otherwise, the agent followed her wordlessly as they made their way towards the generator.

THROUGH A WINDOW DARKLY

Noll caught her stare, narrow and inquisitive, several times, but ignored it.

The way her small fixes went told her the *Taro* would survive. Or at least it wouldn't fall apart on their way to wherever they ended up going. The relief made a part of her click into place—or rather, she clicked into place in something bigger than her. Something important.

She tried not to acknowledge the empty space beside her. *I'm trying, Jayce.*

"I'm sorry for what happened to your brother," Mai said as they moved inside the generator room.

Noll sort of grunted at her. She didn't want to talk. She just wanted to solve the problem so they could progress.

But the woman didn't give up. "You said you...knew me? In your world."

"Yeah." Oh, she was humoring her, great. "Why?"

Mai shrugged. She didn't reply.

"I mean, I don't, not really," Noll elaborated while prying open the generator box. "We met once. Ate dinner in the same room a few times. You're an agent. Sorry, ex-agent. And I'm not, so I wasn't interested."

A faint smile flashed through Mai's face. "I wonder whether there's a world where I'm not one."

This time, Noll was the one who shrugged. Half-forgotten conversations with scientist weirdos about the nature of the universe during various boring clan gatherings on Metallia popped into her head. "I suppose. If there are two or three worlds, there should be more. Infinite, even."

She looked up from inspecting the wires to see Mai squint at her. "You'd think that," the ex-agent said. "But we can't know. Maybe certain things are always the same. Stable points, nails hammered into the multiverse to hold it all together while everything else spins around."

Noll had no idea why they were talking about this. She turned back to the box. A wad of cables bubbled out from the space beyond, some burnt or melted. There was another compartment behind it all, and she could see the silvery casing of the generator tube through the separator film. That part at least seemed intact.

She plugged her tablet into an input to run another diagnostics and started unscrewing gaskets.

"I don't know," she said to fill the silence. Or maybe because she *was* just a bit freaked out about meeting her agent self. "You do seem different than our Mai. Certainly talk more."

Mai laughed. It was a sombre sound but a laugh nonetheless. "It must be because I know you and she doesn't."

She said it like it was obvious. Noll lifted an eyebrow. She suspected the two of them were close, but...this close?

"Anything good you see in me, it's you. I mean, her," Mai added quietly. "Perhaps an anomaly. I don't think I'd get to be like this by my own power."

Noll ignored the tension in her chest and kept working on the cables. "That doesn't make any sense. If we accept there are infinite number of universes, then every possible option needs to happen somewhere. That's just statistics or whatever."

"I know." Mai waved around the flashlight she was supposed to keep fixed to help Noll see. "But think about it. You, the 'yous' that can be paired up with each other in the different universes, must have some immovable, fossilized, unquestionable attributes, right? That makes you *you*. That identifies you, no matter what else changes. It has to be the same in every universe, otherwise it wouldn't be you."

Noll stared at her, incredulous. "You really thought about this a lot, haven't you? Remind me why this matters right now?"

Mai's expression closed, a shadow falling on her frozen features. "Of course, it matters. It matters a lot," she said slowly, every word articulated as if they were painful. "If everything that happens in the multiverse is a collection of all things that *can* happen, and not everything can happen, then this is it. This is all I can be. These are my limits."

Noll pulled her hands out of the box, annoyance getting the better of her. She grabbed onto her jacket, holding herself, frustrated as she faced Mai. "I don't understand. You're just making yourself feel bad while we have more important things to do."

Another wobble of the flashlight beam. Mai's shoulders fell. "It's just...I'm sorry. I needed to tell someone, and—" She halted, thinking. When she spoke again, her voice was softer, and Noll had to lean forward to catch the words. "I did think about this a lot. Ever since we came through, ever since I saw your face and realized what was happening. This changes everything. There are other universes! Doesn't it change everything for you?"

Noll gaped at her. Now, how should she say this? She went for the simplest way she knew. "No. I don't do that. There's already enough bullshit out there. I don't do viewpoint-changing big upheavals."

A faint, empathetic smile appeared on Mai's face. "We kinda had to. You have to understand, I...I liked power. I still like it. I liked to be certain of what I was doing and knowing my actions would be justified by someone above me. Regardless of what was asked of me. That's what I was. What I am. Maybe in every universe. But if you...if Noll saves me, turns me around and pries us out of the clutches of war, maybe then that's okay. Not by my own power, and maybe I don't deserve it, but I can be fine."

Noll had no idea what to say. She really had nothing to do with what the other Noll had or hadn't done to Mai, and this whole thought process was way over her head, and still...

"I didn't save Mai," she muttered. "Our Mai, I mean."

The other woman missed a beat at that, but then her face contorted to a forced smile. She winked. "Not yet. Listen," she went on quickly, seeing Noll's widening eyes, "all I wanted to say was...that I know you.

One of you. And if I'm freaked out, you're freaked out. And you'll want to be brave, but maybe you can't, and it kills you."

"Stars, okay, stop flirting already!" Noll took a step back from her, tried to ignore the nervous tug in her chest. Did she need this now? "I just want to fix this fucking thing—"

"No, wait!" Mai moved towards Noll like she wanted to physically stop her from distancing herself. She was careful not to touch her; she stopped inches away. "That's not— I'm sorry. I was never good with words. I meant that you think what you're doing is not bravery, but sometimes...sometimes we get power from the fear itself. Not from fighting against it. Fear made you doubt working as an agent. Fear helped you get me and Jayce out. We did what we thought was right because even though both sides were scary, we could say we at least tried. The Union fell, not because of us, and it didn't make us better people, but we survived and...we're here."

Noll nodded slowly. "Here as in you schooling me so I don't freak out under pressure and endanger you. Because you think you know me. Is my fear a 'stable point'? Is that who I am, a coward, in every universe? How come you still need me to save you?"

She got so heated by the end of it, and she didn't even know why. This conversation didn't make any sense. She expected Mai to try and defend herself, but she didn't seem like she wanted to as she hung her head and shrugged.

"I don't know. I don't know what to believe. All I know is that you've made it through the worst day of your life once before and made something good out of it. There's no universe where I don't want you to be okay."

Noll stood, paralyzed. This was the most bizarre confession ever. No one had ever talked to her, about her, like this before. This woman had called her a coward and responsible for any ounce of goodness in her with the same breath, and Noll couldn't even yell at her for it because...she kind of understood.

THROUGH A WINDOW DARKLY

And even more, she kind of liked it.

"Well, t-thanks," she muttered, carefully not looking Mai in the eye. "I still think there are infinite universes. And if I save you in some of them, you must be at least a decent person. In some of them. And if you aren't you in some universes, then I'm not me either in some others, but it doesn't mean we can't be good. Or try to be. Plus, who needs their acceptance? We just gotta make it through here and now." The words started out as empty comfort, but as she sounded them out, Noll realized it all rang, in fact, true. "I can't accept the deterministic bullshit, but if you insist, I'll twist it in a way I like."

She turned back to the box, cheeks flaming.

"I know," Mai said. There was a smirk in the comment. The flashlight beam rose again as the ex-agent resumed her position beside her. "That's exactly what I was hoping for. Sorry for...flooding you with this. I don't want to drag Noll— my Noll back into this, although I'm sure she's thinking whatever she's thinking." Noll made a humming sound. Luckily, Mai didn't seem to require more acknowledgement, because she went on. The light beam fell away, making Noll turn to Mai once again, and the woman's eyes gleamed in the dimness, her words smooth but ominous. "And one more thing. Everything I've ever gone through told me the universe doesn't make perfect sense. But at the same time, the universe doesn't make *no sense*, either. And this whole thing we're in the middle of? It feels very fabricated."

Noll swallowed. Mai had some strange theories, but she'd been thinking, hoping, the same thing. "It does, doesn't it?"

Mai nodded. "Before things went to shit, we...the Union had been doing...things to lanes. Some truly terrifying stuff. All that is to say, I agree with your hunch about going to the outskirts."

"Right." Noll swallowed. "Let's go back to this then?"

Mai dropped her shoulders. "Okay. Yes. Let's do that. Thanks. And...sorry."

Noll turned back to the box again. *Oh, man. This is so weird.* "Hey, you know what?" she muttered. "I bet in some random other universe, we're all little blue frogs living happily in a lake on Nefirn-2. You can't prove it's not true, it doesn't sound like the worst fate, and if something, *that* makes me feel better, personally."

She more sensed than saw Mai's sharp expression fold into a smile. The feeling of being stuck in a corner diffused around them. If everything was nonsense, creating any kind of sense was worth it.

Plus, she just got another hunch. That Jayce would like Mai. And the notion also made her feel a bit better.

It took a little more than an hour for them to approach the heliopause of the solar system, spinning the engines as high as Noll dared. Every minute of it was a nail hammered through her fraying hope and sanity. Their repeated scans had not yielded any results around the Window, and all she had to hold onto was some forced logic and her gods damned hunch.

Along the way, Temak returned to consciousness as a result of the agents'—okay, ex-agents—diligent tending to him. Noll helped him sit and lean against the inner hull while Liepok unwrapped another ultra-modern medpack to have it at the ready.

"Welcome back, soldier." Noll made her voice as light as she could. Temak's eyes focused on her, and his gaze cleared. She forced a smile on her face. "You won't believe the news."

"Are we safe?" he drawled.

Noll glanced behind her where Noll-2 and Mai sat at the dashboard, keeping their eyes on things. "Interesting question. We

THROUGH A WINDOW DARKLY

think we're in a parallel universe, there's another one of me in this cockpit with us right now, and we're heading off to see some exotic radiation at the outskirts of the solar system. What do you think?"

Temak leaned to the side, following her gaze. Noll-2 and Mai looked his way for a short second, but it was enough or Temak's eyes to go wide and nervously shift back to Noll. "Is this for real?"

"Yep."

"Am I dead?"

"No, but I feel you."

The man pulled himself upright, trying out motion with his limbs, finding them in a good enough state that he ended up flexing with a pleased expression. As he looked back at Noll with a faint smirk, she could be sure he was feeling much better. "Well. One is more than enough of you, but I think I can deal."

Noll frowned. "You sure you wanna go there after you almost shot me dead, pretty boy?"

Immediate guilt consumed Temak's expression. His eyes shifted to Liepok who hadn't been talking, just sitting on their haunches beside the two of them. He seemed to shrink, although he didn't change is posture. "I'm sorry. Again. I acted horribly. Something just...clicked in my brain. There's no excuse for it, and I don't have the right to ask you to trust me again..."

He fell silent. Noll didn't break the quiet, deciding to wait for Liepok. The Nefirn thought for a while, and then they reached out, placing a hand on Temak's shoulder. "You were afraid. I understand fear."

"I wasn't—" Temak stopped himself with a sigh. He closed his eyes for a second. "No, I was. It made me stupid. I won't do it again."

"We'll hold each other, even being afraid," Liepok said quietly.

At Temak's questioning look, Noll gave a wink. "Metaphorically, of course."

Temak nodded. "Of course." His eye glinted with humor, his gaze not moving from Noll for a second.

Bastard. Noll decided to ignore the tingle in her stomach. "So, to catch you up..."

Later, Noll even managed to regain control over her ship, leaving the doppelganger and Mai to answer Temak's remaining inquiries while Liepok played the calming presence and the lightning rod in the middle. Thankfully, that didn't have to last long, although everyone was strangely amiable. They were getting close.

As the *Taro* propelled its way through the void across the final leg of the journey—space really was 99% boredom 1% 'fuck we're gonna die', wasn't it?—she pulled up data on the Duplex system on another hunch. She frowned at it for a few seconds. Noll-2 stepped beside her, following her stare and scanning the screen.

"Something wrong?" she asked.

Temak hobbled over, squinting at the screens. "You said this is a parallel universe, right? If we're still in the Duplex system, where are the planets?"

"Exactly," Noll said. "The central star has the same attributes as back home, but Duplex itself is obviously not where it should be, and according to this info and my own very recent memories, there should be two gas giants orbiting somewhere around here." Noll waved at the long-range radar, distinctly empty of any kind of planetary signals. "And there's nothing."

"Maybe they never existed here," Liepok pondered. When everyone turned to them, they seemed to diminish in size like they didn't want all the attention. "That's what it looks like."

It was probably a more plausible explanation than someone exploding them out of existence. But Noll didn't feel like wondering how planet formation had apparently proceeded in an entirely different fashion in this solar system billions of years ago while the Window

THROUGH A WINDOW DARKLY

itself was seemingly in the same place, so she swiped the info away and focused on the radiation wall again.

"Numbers are definitely weird," she commented. The computer spat out results reluctantly, as if it didn't want to confirm anything prematurely. Whatever surrounded this solar system from all sides was anomalous and deeply out of place.

They all leaned over the screens as the *Taro* closed in on the whatever-the-fuck; Noll in the pilot seat, Liepok beside her, and the two agents with Temak standing behind. Judging from the energy flux, they should have already seen something—Noll imagined a structure of some kind or a strange cloud, but the ship was heading into nothing but darkness for now. Darkness and...

"Umm," Noll-2 said, her voice shaking. "The stars look a bit different tonight."

Good gods. How had she not noticed it before? None of them had. Silent horror clenched Noll's jaw shut. Sure, the starry sky was a beautiful sight that accompanied the wayward lanehunter everywhere they wandered, but when you frequently ran for your life, it was only important as long as you determined you wouldn't collide with a moon or a swarm of asteroids while scurrying away from and possibly also towards trouble.

But scanning the view again, it was obvious. This was not the usual empty space scattered with sparkling stars around them. No, those small blue dots were not distant, flaming gas balls at all. As the *Taro* approached the radiation signal, they didn't even look like spots of light anymore. They looked like close-by, thin, jagged lines.

Lines crossing each other, forming a spider web of bright blue chasms. Suddenly, Noll knew exactly what she was looking at.

Lanes.

Thousands and thousands of thin tears in spacetime, hairline breaks in the monumental, darkened wall of the universe. The lights they'd thought to be stars were the spots where more of them crisscrossed each other either physically or in perspective. As the *Taro* sped ahead, the spiderweb network grew and came into focus, the lanes widening, the gaps between them closing in, milky fog seeping out to envelop the view in an unsettling haze. There was barely any normal space left out here. The computer feverishly tried to detect and categorize each and every break, but there were millions, billions, as far as the scans could penetrate.

There weren't any stars. There were just the lanes and cracks, smaller, larger, in a dense tangle, gleaming brilliantly. Everywhere.

More cracks than wall.

Noll felt cold sweat pour down her face. This was not possible. In her universe, the normal universe, there were maybe a dozen systems that looked like this—so broken up by lanes it was hard to even traverse them. As soon as you left one lane, you tended to drop into another. They were so densely webbed that every star, every planet had already broken apart into atoms inside them.

But those were rare. She'd never seen anything like this before. But all these lanes were in every direction, apparently, and they were...moving in?

"What happened here?" Noll-2 asked in a whisper. "Is everything...is the whole universe like this?"

"That's stupid." Noll didn't want to think about it. "That's not possible."

It was also clear that whatever she hoped they could get out of this journey wasn't going to happen. The whole trip was useless. The panic slithered back across the edges of her vision.

Jayce, where are you? Are you...are you dead?

She swallowed, static enveloping her view. "I'm just going to turn around now, if you agree." Not even on her better days would she be eager to start crossing a region like this. If they fell into one of these lanes, they'd end up somewhere else deep into this spiderweb. They'd

THROUGH A WINDOW DARKLY

get torn apart by tidal forces before they could even lose all hope for finding their way out.

Everyone was silent as she typed in the commands to change their trajectory. She couldn't wait to be far, far away from here.

But the *Taro* didn't move as she expected. And by the time she realized the ship had been steadily accelerating during the last minute or so, even though she hadn't boosted the thrust, they were plummeting towards the closest lane with increasing velocity.

"Shit," she hissed. "Shit, shit, shit, everyone hold on to something!"

And they all did, although it didn't help much, neither her desperate attempts to course-correct. A gravitational potential well the strength of a black hole's twisted them around and pulled them in, much stronger than what Noll had ever experienced around lanes. They tumbled, the entire ship shaking like a tin can of loose screws. Everyone yelled at Noll to turn them around as the nearest gap in space started to fill their screen, but there was nothing she could do. The *Taro* was doing maximum thrust, and it was not enough.

As darkness dawned to sharp blue light around them, they dropped into the lane like a pebble thrown into a rushing river.

"For fuck's sake, turn around!" Mai grabbed her shoulder like that could help.

Status warnings swarmed the screens, and the instruments went wild. As they crossed the barrier between normal and anomalous space-time, Noll's stomach jumped into her throat, and gravity turned upside down for a dizzying second.

"Feel free to take over if you think you can do better!"

Mai didn't take over. Noll typed in another row of commands, trying to calculate a safe vector as they free-fell through the void. But something was wrong. Numbers scrolled into infinity in front of her, and there was no safe vector. There was no safe way out.

There's always a way! There's always a vector! her brain screamed. But that was not true. Noll just never went into lanes where there wasn't.

The hull whined, the lights flickering. There was nothing on the screens except infinite blue void. Exotic particles shore against the shields, the temperature and pressure rising beyond acceptable values. The *Taro* couldn't bear this strain for long. Something growled in the tail section like an angry wolf. *Bad noise. Very bad.*

Noll reached out to grab Liepok's hand, and the Nefirn squeezed her fingers. She twisted around to look at the others. There was true terror on her doppelganger's face; Mai clung to Noll-2 like she'd never let go; Temak's warm brown eyes fixed on her, a kind of peace in them.

She closed her eyes. This was it, then. *Fuck me. I still wanted to—*

And then silence. And then darkness. Her eyes snapped open. It was dark outside on the screens, and calm. All readings dropped back to normal. Like a giant's hand had plucked the *Taro* out of the flood and put them into their giant pocket.

"What the—" Noll-2 fell silent, sounding as confused as Noll felt.

Noll flicked the brake thrusters on, and a good thing she did, because as they slowed, environmental scans popped up on the main screen. They were in a large cavern of a sort, far from the heliopause as much as Noll could see on the radars. The place was artificial, angular, made of some strong metal alloy the scans couldn't identify. A dock inside a space station? Not far behind the *Taro's* tail, the brilliant blue of a teeny tiny crack shone in the dark. A small lane inside the strange structure.

Noll turned the engine off and leaned back in the pilot seat, chest buzzing, vision sharp. Noll-2 and Mai heaved, bracing against the dashboard to calm down. Liepok just sat, face whiter than Noll had ever seen it, frozen.

"Where...where are we now?" Temak asked behind her, tone flat.

Noll inhaled. Yes, good question. Questions had answers, sometimes, so she ran another scan. Her eyes went wide looking at the results. "I don't know, but there's a humongous energy signal coming from the middle of this structure." How had they not seen this before? Were they even in the same solar system?

Mai ran a hand over her face and brushed close beside Noll to inspect the numbers. "It's similar to what we detected when the Window changed. I'm pretty sure." She glanced down at a tablet in her hand Noll hadn't noticed before. She swiped across its display a few times. "There are life signs, too. From another section, but it's clear as day."

Noll blinked. Life signs. *Life signs.*

"How many?" Liepok asked.

Mai didn't answer. It was Noll-2 who inclined her head towards the tablet, her voice as shaky as before. "This thing is pretty smart, but not very sensitive. They're too far away. But...they're there."

Noll almost heard the door open. That horrible door she'd nearly just eased shut.

Jayce.

He was alive.

7

"It's them," Noll whispered. "It has to be them."

The same hope glinted in her doppelganger's eyes as she smiled faintly at her. They'd just been saved by someone or something moments before inevitable death. That someone might have also brought their lost people here before their oxygen ran out.

It wasn't such a crazy supposition, considering everything else they'd gone through here.

"Right. Let's not be hasty." Mai scowled at her tablet as if she could pry more info out of the blinking dots with the sheer power of her mind. "We might run into those that did this to us."

"Maybe," Noll said. She tried to breathe evenly, but her heart clattered around in her chest in a frenzy. "Would that be such a bad thing?" Temak grunted disapprovingly at her ominous tone, so she added, "We need to see this through. This is our best clue yet."

"Clue?" Temak glared at her. "We've been brought here against all odds. It's a trap, not a clue."

Deep silence followed. No one moved an inch, everyone seemingly chewing on their non-existing options in their heads. Noll had a hard time focusing on anything else that wasn't the renewed jittering in her body, but before her impatience could have risen above the fear, it was Liepok who spoke again. "There's not much else we can do."

There was such determination in the thin voice, even though Liepok still seemed breathless after their near-death experience. Noll squinted at Temak and Mai. "They're right. We might find those we lost. We have to try."

Mai nodded first, sneaking a glance at her Noll, as usual. Temak didn't relent, fear glinting in his eyes, until Noll faced him and lightly touched his wrist. He looked at her, wary.

"I know," she said quietly. "I'm afraid, too. But I trust you." She shrugged. "I mean, I think. As long as your gun is not directed at me."

Temak's mouth curled up a smidge. "I'll never live that down, will I?"

"Nope. Will you help me?"

"Do I dare not?"

He actually winked. The fear wasn't gone from his glance, and from Noll's chest either, but it helped a little.

Noll turned back to Mai and waved at the tablet in her hands. There was no time to waste. "We can circle around the structure, get closer to them."

Following Mai's instructions and the *Taro's* scans, they navigated out of the dock-like cavern and coasted around the station. The structure was shaped roughly like a cube, made of some pale grey metal none of them recognized, and was as large as a decent-sized city. The surfaces were sleek and smooth, corners sharp like bone here but rounded over there, with details materializing when they drifted closer. Compartments connected with tunnels and bridges; tiny docked vehicles waited motionlessly in endless rows; oval dents peppered vast surfaces Noll couldn't even guess the function of. The construction didn't resemble neither Union nor lanehunter architecture, and none of the alien worlds Noll or Temak knew built stuff like this either. It could have been Talalan, maybe, but only because no one saw much of how their structures looked like.

Perhaps it was made by some unknown-to-them civilization. If the history of this universe differed from theirs, it was possible. Dangers Noll couldn't even imagine might exist hidden inside of it.

Was Jayce here? Were those life signs really him, and the Krotkes, and the Nefirns? Or just bait?

They found a second dock, another jagged bite mark along one of the cube edges on the opposite side of where they'd been before, as close to the life signs as they could get. Noll's apprehension gathered as

THROUGH A WINDOW DARKLY

she started the landing process. The airlocks of the station were made to accept standard lanehunter docking mechanisms which made her job easier but was disconcerting, too.

They filed out of the airlock one by one, armed and as prepared as they'd ever be, and soon found themselves on an empty, white-green hallway. There was no sound, no movement around them as Noll sealed the *Taro*, hoping it wasn't the last time she saw her dear ship. The five of them exchanged a morose look and moved forward together, carefully, into the bowels of the station.

Triangular lights at regular intervals on the walls illuminated their way, flickering intermittently. As they progressed, a low, droning sound emanating from somewhere became louder and louder in the background, but apart from that, they heard nothing, saw no one. Air circulation and heating obviously worked; they passed many, many closed doors, but they didn't meet a soul.

Mai walked at the front alongside the other Noll, the two of them like symmetrical parts of a well-oiled machine, sneaking forward to peer around corners and scan the shit out of everything before Liepok, Temak, and Noll got close. The Nefirn themself walked like half their brain was stuck in a nightmare—Noll had given them a plasma gun, but they looked as natural with it as if she'd hung it onto a tree branch. In a life-death situation, they'd be *so* toast.

Temak seemed balanced, for once. He kept up with her and Liepok, covering their backs, focused. A comforting presence. Noll smirked to herself. Jayce would probably chide her for feeling...affection, or whatever this was—the man had pulled a gun on her, after all—but she couldn't help it.

Well. He can play the protective brother for a bit when I finally found him.

Terror was still drumming in her skull, but from time to time, hope chimed in, too. Then terror again. It was a whole damn jam session in there, so loud she could barely hear her own thoughts.

"This is a labyrinth," Mai grumbled when ten minutes went by, and they were getting nowhere. The hallways wove around, uniform, unchanging, with the same white-and-green aesthetics as before. Sometimes the group passed through wider rooms that seemed like community areas, maybe, but every door opening from them were sealed, just like those on the hallways. They found nothing they knew the function of, nothing that pointed further than "table", "chair", or "decoration, maybe, question mark?" If Noll wanted to, she could have gotten into a switchboard behind one of those suspicious square-shaped imprints on the wall she noted from time to time, but the life signs were getting closer and closer on Mai's tablet. They were almost there.

"Who built this?" Liepok pondered as they followed Noll around another corner. "And why?"

Temak shrugged. "Trade. Habitat. Military station. Communication. Anything, really."

If Noll's newest hunch was right, what they'd seen out there implied that in this universe, this solar system was the only place left. It sure seemed like it was just lanes all the way down everywhere else. This was everything: a star, the Window, and this station.

Sure, they couldn't be sure. Maybe there were other places. Somewhere. Her hunch did not agree with the thought, though. She was starting to like the hunch less and less, too. It was usually Jayce's thing anyway. Like she was unconsciously trying to replicate this aspect of him while he was gone from her side, and she was not going there. Not now.

"The real question is, why is it here?" she said. "Why is it *still* here?"

"Shush. We're getting closer," the other her interrupted.

Noll grasped her gun more tightly, and they watched Noll-2 scout ahead. It was still eerie how much her doppelganger moved like her. Smoother and more careful—the military training was obvious—but in rare moments when she was distracted, it was like staring into the twisted mirror again.

Then Noll-2 squinted back at her, and Noll was flooded with empathy. Both of them just wanted their brothers back.

They continued to sneak forth. At a T intersection, Mai pointed to the left, and they abided until they reached the end of the hallway: a closed metal door.

"That sucks," Noll said. "You sure it's this way?"

The two ex-agents nodded. Noll-2 plopped the small backpack she'd brought onto the ground, crouched, and rummaged through it to pull out a small metallic tool from what looked like a stashed belt. Without a word, she started twiddling around with it at the door lock.

Noll scoffed. *Agents and their tricks...*

She kept an eye out backwards alongside Temak while her twin worked, lest some enigmatic alien attacker surprised them. Mai looked over her Noll with careful eyes, and Liepok...well, they were listening.

And listening even harder, their eyes wide. They stumbled to the closed door and fell on their knees, hands splayed against the surface, almost pushing Noll-2 out of the way. The woman drew back with an impolite grunt, but Liepok wasn't paying attention; they just yelled out, much louder than Noll would have thought they could. "Frahyss!"

Noll only recognized the word because she'd heard it before. It was the name of the Nefirn captain, but the flood of words that followed eluded her—Liepok was speaking to their suprior, their friend, as if they were standing on the other side of the door.

"Li?"

The quick, endlessly spooling words out of Liepok's mouth drained reluctantly as they turned to her. Their expression didn't change, but every single line on their face deepened. "They're in there," they said, their voice faltering in excitement. "I can hear them...can you hear them?"

Mai scowled real hard; she obviously couldn't hear anything. But Noll didn't waste a second. She crouched beside Liepok, her ear to the door.

"Jayce..." she whispered. *He isn't going to hear this, stupid.* But she couldn't make herself speak louder around the weird ball of gum in her throat.

She could have sworn there was a dull thump from the other side. Steps? Knocks? She couldn't decide.

"Noll? Noll!"

She flattened against the door, both palms at it, yelling now. "JAYCE! I'm here! It's me! We're gonna get you out of here, okay?"

"Noll, for fuck's sake!" Her twin brother's voice was barely audible through all that damn metal. "I thought I'd never see you again!"

He's there. He's here! She couldn't talk. Everything crystallized, the present contouring itself against her fading panic. Jayce was alive.

Her brother didn't wait for her brain to catch up. "How the fuck did you find me? What the fuck happened?" he shouted.

Noll felt the salt of her tears on her tongue. It was his voice, his words from behind the door where he was maybe leaning against it just like Noll was. He was there. Breathing. Alive. And she was going to embrace him in a few seconds if the other her could finally—

She glanced to the side, and their eyes met. Tears were flowing down Noll-2's face, too, but she wiped away the mess with a second of delay to attack the lock again with renewed fervor.

There was another sound from the other side, then Nefirn words again. Liepok answered so sharply beside her that it hurt her ears. She hadn't seen them this alive since they'd met. Noll-2 sniffled at the lock, still working. A hand clasped onto Noll's shoulder—Temak. She squeezed his fingers, not looking back.

Almost there. Almost.

"Noll, we're never going to Duplex again. I don't care how cheap Saori sells Rixian rum. I'm not risking this shit, I swear."

THROUGH A WINDOW DARKLY

She laughed through the snot and tears. Jayce's tone was ridiculously whiny, but there was humor in it. Like when he'd burst into their tiny flat, ranting about some character who tried to double-cross him, or begged to Noll through fake tears to accompany him to some planet or else following his newest obsession.

He was alive.

He is alive.

It felt like a millennium until the other Noll finally reared back from the lock, and with impetus, shoved the door in. Noll and Liepok stood, both out of balance, wavering.

Around twenty people faced them, clumped together in an otherwise empty room on the other side. Mostly Nefirn faces, a few human that were familiar, but at that point, Noll wasn't even looking at them anymore because there was only one she was looking for. And he was there, scared, worn, frustrated, grinning. There was a single short burst of thought: *is it even him?* but then she was sure, and she ran at him to close him in an embrace so tight his bones must have been cracking under it.

"Ouch," Jayce complained weakly, but he hugged her back, burying his face in Noll's neck for a long, long moment.

She didn't want to let go. This was a miracle.

It only hit her now, but she'd lost hope. She had. Sure, it had been buzzing around her like an ugly, bloodsucking mosquito swooping down at the most unfitting moments to drain life out of her until she slapped it away with a palm. She had to go on, because she would have never forgiven herself for not doing everything she could to find him, but she'd accepted it, somewhere deep. That this was it. That she'd be alone from now on; it was gonna be her, half of a person, for the rest of her life. And it would always hurt, the crater of absence in the middle of her being, but she'd go on, limping like she'd lost a leg, heaving like her very lungs were blown off, not giving up only because Jayce wouldn't want her to.

Now everything was whole again, and it hit her with the force of a hurricane. It didn't even matter where they were or why. They got this. She could finally breathe again.

Then the outside world started filtering in, and Jayce's squeeze slowly loosened. He leaned away, locking eyes with her. His hair was hanging limp, his skin pallid and sweaty. "You okay? How are you here? Where is here? Can we leave? Do you know what in all hells is going on?"

"I...don't," Noll replied, sniffing. Neither of them had ever been the hugging type, but it felt impossible to cut physical contact right now. She reached out to sweep the hair off of Jayce's forehead. "Lane bullshit. Parallel worlds. I met...myself. I suppose you did too?"

Jayce frowned. "Oh yeah. It's been, like, *so* weird. How did you find us?"

Noll just shook her head. How could she even start to explain? Luck? Fate? Blind chance? Someone playing them like little chess figures on a vast board?

"Your jacket's torn," Jayce muttered, tapping at a small hole in the material at Noll's collarbone. She glanced down. It must have gotten caught in something when the nailship's hit pushed her over the *Taro's* console. The material was too thin; she'd had the jacket since forever. "You love this thing. Are you alright?"

Her chest constricted, and she held him closer. "No? Yes?"

She chuckled self-consciously. Jayce snorted, squeezing her arm a bit tighter. "Yeah. I know. We're okay now."

His stare found something behind Noll, and settled as if he just couldn't look away. She turned to see Noll-2 and her brother stand there, talking quietly, holding each other in much the same way as they did. Mai stood close, her eyes wet. Behind those three, Liepok was in the ring of five Nefirns, wrapped up in deep conversation with all of them, it seemed like. Not too far from that group, the same five Nefirns milled about, a bit uncertain but looking relieved. Noll blinked. What a strange optical illusion.

Temak drifted about on the outskirts of the room. He had no one here. Noll let go of Jayce for a second to grab his wrist and pull him in.

"I know you!" Jayce welcomed him. "You're that spy!"

"A lousy one." The man gave a faint grin and introduced himself.

Noll poked him in the side. "None of this talk. You came to help us, and that's worth more."

She expected the next four figures who stepped up to them, but it didn't help with the momentary disorientation: it was the Krotke twins, doubled.

"Um," Ruis-1 started. Ruis-2, two feet behind him, grimaced, fingers massaging his temples, probably not for the first time that day. "So, this is fucked up. Please tell me: did we do this?"

"No, you donut." Rolte-1 lightly whacked a hand against the nape of his neck. Then, hesitating, he looked at Noll, too. "Did we?"

Noll couldn't help but snort-laugh so hard it almost hurt. An ugly sound rumbled out from the depths of her, then it was seconds later, and she was still cackling, clinging at Jayce's arm and dabbing at her aggressively watering eyes, and it just wouldn't stop...but by that time, at least the others were laughing as well, her twin's heaving chortle the loudest of them all.

One by one, they managed to curb the madness. Noll turned to Jayce to ask how in hells had they gotten to this station without suffocating in space after all, the thought of how they'd get back to their respective universes entering her mind for the first time, when there was a crackle and a long static sound from somewhere above their heads. Temak drew his gun, but it was just a loudspeaker or comm system they couldn't see emitting distorted, choppy sentences that echoed through the room.

"Oh, wonderful! You found each other. That's great! Please, join me on the bridge of the station. I might be able to help you get home."

I'll be waiting here. Not that...not that I can do anything else, haha..." The cheerful speech devolved into an awkward laugh, but then the voice went on. "Please. I'd like to apologize. And explain."

Then there was a loud click, and the comms disconnected.

Everyone was strangely calm as they got ready to face whoever they needed to face. Liepok told and re-told the Nefirns the story of how they'd come through the Window with the *Taro*—in both groups only a few spoke Common well, so they mostly used their own language. The other Nefirns, the ones from Mai and Noll-2's universe, were wary of the tale in lack of their own Liepok who had not come through, but they of course couldn't not believe their eyes. It didn't seem like they'd ever buddied up with their doppelgangers during the time spent here—the Krotkes and Jayce were the only ones with a casual enough attitude about it.

"I don't trust this," Mai said. They all stood in a circle tallying up their belongings, distributing weapons, tools, and some food and water among those who needed it the most. Jayce and Jayce-2 had recounted how, after the Window had pulled them through, they only floated in space for a second when some kind of tractor beam had caught them and transported them to the station through a small lane. That happened for the two groups separately, but since then, they'd all either been unconscious from the shock to their system, or cooped up in this room, and this was the first time they had any communication from the entity in command of the place.

"He, they, whatever, never spoke to us." Jayce-2 shrugged. He looked exactly like Noll's Jayce, except his hair was longer and darker.

THROUGH A WINDOW DARKLY

"There was some weird nutribar-like food here when we first came to, and water, but..."

"...he, they, never showed themself," Jayce finished his sentence. The two of them took pleasure in doing that as often as they could. "I guess now that y'all are here, too, they can't put it off anymore?"

"Or it's a trap," Mai added.

"Whoever it is, they did sound pretty strange," Temak agreed. "Apologize, they said? I'd like to hear it."

"Plus," Jayce-2 said, "I wouldn't say no to some help to get back. What was happening to the Window when you guys last saw it?"

Noll looked at the other her. With the intense emotions of the reunion subsiding, her thoughts were quickly turning darker, and she couldn't help but wonder whether she was alone with that. "I think it was still leading to our world, but it could have changed since," Noll-2 said. "Especially if these people or this person is controlling it."

"But why?" Liepok asked, somewhat frustrated. "What's the goal? They sounded confused."

Noll-2 shrugged. "Like they made a mistake? Yeah. We'll see it soon."

That's mild, Noll thought with anger stirring in her stomach. Didn't she wish for revenge? It was all she could think of now.

"But what if it *is* a trap?" Mai repeated. Seemed like at least she'd regained some old-fashioned pessimism.

But thinking like that would just hold them back. "If it is, we're already caught," Noll replied. "We're on their station, near vulnerable. What we can do is to try and get some answers. Find those responsible and hold them responsible. Together."

Everyone blinked uneasily but didn't argue in the end. Noll sent a faint smile as a reaction to Liepok's worried glance. They were all together in this. Had to get to the end of the road somehow.

"Okay." Temak sighed. "Let's finish this."

The agents walked in front of everyone, then the Nefirns and the Krotkes with Jayce and Noll (times two) behind, and Temak closing the little procession. Easily twenty people and the most bizarre group ever, that was how they marched through the empty station following Mai's directions to the energy signal they'd seen before, supposing that was where their secretive host resided. They continued to not bump into anyone at all. The place was completely empty, booming from loneliness. If there was a community living and thriving here at some point, it had been gone a long, long time ago.

Jayce didn't let go of Noll's hand for a second. Noll wasn't sure whether it was because he wanted to protect her or because he needed to feel safe, but it was probably both, and honestly, she wasn't going to let go either. Hope and foreboding fought for dominance in her mind.

"When this is over," her brother said quietly, "we go on vacation. To one of those boring-ass places you're always longing for. At least for a day or two, I swear."

Noll snorted. Jayce knew his boundaries, at least. Two days at best, and only if he *really* tried to stay put. That was all the vacation they were going to get, and they both knew it.

"I'll hold you to it," she said anyway. "If we get out of this."

Jayce smirked. "We will. We always do."

"Jinx."

"Double jinx."

She squeezed his hand. Then they made their way into the large room Mai indicated was their end goal.

It looked like the bridge of a huge spaceship. A deck-to-ceiling window on the opposite wall showed some jutting-out sections of the cube-station with the star-scattered (lane-scattered) void in the background. It must have been some sort of screen, judging from the labels and numbers appearing in one corner—some kind of status report, but Noll didn't immediately understand the details. In front of it, in the middle of the room, a large sphere of brilliant white light

THROUGH A WINDOW DARKLY

hung from the ceiling surrounded by a machine with arms and strange manipulators. Below, a circular console stood with a myriad of buttons and displays—the impression was, whatever the sphere did, it could be controlled with the console. The rest of the room was packed dense with server towers, memory cubes, and processor stacks with two short staircases leading to a circular mezzanine. Up there, the view was more of the same: computers and mystifying devices galore.

The air was cool with a constant, gentle breeze. The droning sound they'd caught before was the loudest in there thus far, but not so bad they couldn't hear each other above it. In its heyday, probably thirty, forty people must have worked in this space, judging from the number of workstations. Now it was empty, apart from a single person.

A lanky figure rose from a chair at the central console. As Noll's entire group filed in, cautious and wary, the stranger walked towards them; in the milky light of the weird device above, their face was only clear when they stood merely at a few steps' distance. From the fine dark grey spiderweb pattern on their face, it was obvious they were Talalan.

Noll squinted at Temak. The man lifted an eyebrow, his face otherwise flat. Not paranoid, just cautious.

"Thank you for coming here," the stranger spoke up. Their voice was weak but echo-y in the large room, rising easily above the low hum. As they took another step forward, their movements were choppy like they hadn't full control over them. Their white hair was sparse, and they were thin as if starving. Like their body wanted to fall apart into pieces similarly to their entire lane-crisscrossed universe around them.

They were not old, Noll thought. Tired. Maybe sick.

"I'm so very, *very* sorry about what happened," they said. "This was not my intention at all."

"Then pray tell what *was* your intention?" Noll asked through her clenched jaw. She hadn't planned to talk, but she couldn't help it: her anger flared up like a red giant locked into her chest. Jayce held her hand, steady, and Temak stepped up beside her.

The Talalan seemed to catch the tension and backed off a step. Mai took over in a more level voice. "Who are you? Why did you do this to us?"

The Talalan looked over the group. Noll tried to see through her indignation. A single alien sure wasn't what she'd expected. They were all alone in here, and like before, they were apologizing. They had no weapons; they were barely standing on their feet.

"My name is Firl. Please, believe me when I say, I am truly sorry. I was only trying to save what could be saved."

Silence. Temak gave a large, theatrical sigh. "What does that mean? Would you start from the beginning?"

Firl blinked, taken aback. "I will. I will tell you. I failed in my ventures, obviously, but I think I kind of succeeded, too. At least I hope so. Is everyone alright? Does any of you need assistance?"

The group-murmur rose a notch or two. "We're fine. Not counting the incidental physical and mental trauma," Jayce said nonchalantly. His doppelganger snickered. "So, tell us. What's this whole shebang? You alone here?"

The Talalan nodded. "I'm the last sentient thing alive in this whole universe."

The mutterings immediately ceased. One of the Nefirns shuffled around. *Oh gods, they don't even understand most of this.* Noll hoped Liepok had the presence of mind to translate.

"You've been there. You saw it. This place is doomed. I tried to hold out as long as I could. I hoped..." Firl fell silent. It was as if they'd noticed the group for the first time, really noticed it, registering that they were talking to someone and not just reciting some practiced speech.

THROUGH A WINDOW DARKLY

Their legs buckled, and they backed off to let themselves back into their chair. Their next sigh was deep like all the air was leaving their lungs, trying to propel out something poisonous from deep inside.

"Nine years, three months, two days. In Talalan timekeeping. That's how long I've been alone, trying to reach some kind of breakthrough with the Window." They looked up at the group. "And I did it."

"Stars. What happened to you?" Mai asked. She wanted meaning so badly. Would she find it in the end?

Firl cleared their throat and nodded, giving themself permission to talk. "There was a war. There's always a war. In your worlds, too. I see agents, lanehunters among you—that's how it started. A horrible period, absolutely avoidable if we'd have looked farther than our own shadows, but...we survived. We got through it, and we thought we'd gotten smart enough to avoid it forever. But pretty soon, everyone started to fiddle with the lanes, and no one had the presence of mind to say 'stop it!' Stop being afraid and work with each other. Stop giving into fear!"

Noll's chest ached. She was frozen still, had trouble focusing on the present. Because it was the same story, wasn't it? Almost happened in her world, too, if the gossip was true. Someone wanted to use the lanes as energy sources, open new ones and experiment, which made everyone else seize up in terror and scramble to do something before that something was done to them. And yes, catastrophe had been avoided, but who knew how close they'd gotten?

She didn't know. It was all so far above her. She could do nothing but watch and listen.

"But it turned even worse than that," the Talalan went on. "Lanes were weaponized. Whole systems were eradicated, entire regions of spacetime corrupted into open, bleeding wounds of singularities. They were spreading fast, unstoppable. By the time the warring sides noticed they were killing themselves, it was over. The chain reaction we'd been afraid of had come to pass, and the universe was devouring itself."

A whole reality, gone. Noll ground her teeth. Jayce's hands squeezed around her fingers, holding her back from toppling over the precipice.

Firl looked up. Their voice implied tears, but they weren't crying—maybe they had been over that for a long time now. The story continued to flood out of their mouth. "The Window has always been more stable than the other lanes. It was our best chance to break into the multiverse. When the chain reaction became an open secret, those who wanted to fight for our world came here to try the impossible. No one ever reached through parallel worlds before, even though we knew they existed. Back then, we realized they were our one chance to survive. We held on and kept trying, me and my compatriots, in the middle of this impossible destruction. After all, we started the whole thing."

"What do you mean?"

Firl glanced at Noll-2. "We started the experimenting. Us, Talalans. We made the first prototypes and failed to destroy them when caught. It was...too tempting. The mystery of where the lanes came from and why, and what we can do with them. A long time ago, our curiosity had almost eradicated our whole race. Looks like we never learned. This time, our irresponsibility killed the universe. Somehow, you never really believe..." They trailed off, their gaze shifting at the white sphere above, their face deadly pale now as they forced the words out. "You never believe that what you do can have such a large effect on the world. But it does. It does. For better or worse."

Noll swallowed. Her eyes found Liepok's. The Nefirn stood close to Captain Frahyss, their posture tense but firm. 'Taking it in a stride' would have probably been an overstatement, but they were holding on.

"Then, one by one, everyone died. Five of us remained." Firl sighed. "Then just me. I'm doing one thing and one thing only, now. I keep the system stable with the device while working on my theory to open the Window to other universes." A strange smile appeared on their face.

THROUGH A WINDOW DARKLY

"Not to run away, anymore. Just to warn you all. And I managed! I can barely believe I lived to see you!"

"And what would you warn us about?" Jayce grunted. His tone was gruff; Firl's story had left its mark on him, but he tried valiantly. "That lanes are dangerous? Thanks, we know."

Firl stared at him, the smile melting off their face. They opened their mouth. Then they closed it. The grin returned, tired, uncertain. "No, you're right. I always thought if I get to this point, meeting someone from another reality, I'd say something grandiose and deep. 'You must unite and conquer fear or you'll end up like us', or 'Your fate is still in your hands, learn from our mistake and save yourselves!' But...you're right. What can I say that you don't know already? We knew where we were going. Sentients are very good at ignoring every warning sign until they feel the burn on their own body. Even then, we move slowly."

Noll swallowed. Her vision swarmed with white and grey dots, and her legs felt like jelly. She didn't want to listen to this. She couldn't. Was there no sense in what had happened to them? She'd almost just died, body and mind smeared over light-years and light-years of twisted, broken space-time, and for what? There was no answer. Mai was wrong. Sometimes things didn't make sense at all. Sometimes, everything was hopelessly fragmented.

How many universes had done this to themselves? How long until Noll's would do it too? Was this the end? How could anyone stand up to the powers high above, so greedy and scared and blinded?

Was the extinction of sentience unavoidable? Wouldn't that be just the most horrible thing that had ever occurred to her in her entire life?

She heard Firl's closing words muffled through her panic. "Sadly, the Window still doesn't work exactly how I want it to. It made a connection with one universe but slipped to several neighbouring ones without my sayso. And of course, the connection was much more violent than I planned—that's why you're here."

"Why didn't you talk to us first? Why did you wait until we got lost out there?" Temak asked.

Firl glanced to the deck. "I wasn't...I wasn't sure what to do at first. I saved the first group, but I panicked. I was preparing for this, but I still wasn't sure how to go about it. Then the machine malfunctioned, pulled through more. You were...shooting at each other. I didn't know what to do."

Temak scowled. "You have a whole space station!"

"A research station, yes. I have no weapons!" Firl's indignant, offended voice dropped, then they sighed. "In any case, I think I can do it again. It will be easier with you here; you all have such clear energy imprints on you. I'm pretty sure I can send all of you home."

"Do you think we can do it?" Mai asked unexpectedly. Like she hadn't even heard the last sentences. "Is there a universe that isn't rushing to its doom? Is the collapse unavoidable?"

If there were infinite universes, everything could happen. But Noll was even less sure than before. How could they know whether they only had a determined number of fates? And how was this knowledge, that the worst thing had already happened to another reality, was even surviveable?

"Nothing is inevitable," Firl replied. Their voice was certain now, driven. "Nothing is deterministic. The smallest pebble matters, because it makes waves on the lake. If it matters towards destruction, it matters towards healing."

Mai nodded slowly, hugging herself like she was cold. Noll-2 moved closer to her protectively.

Stars. Was this really enough for them?

"Bullshit," Noll heard herself say. "We don't make waves. We make nothing. We're nothing."

Cold quiet followed her words. She wavered on her feet, even though Jayce was still holding her.

"Noll..." That was Mai.

THROUGH A WINDOW DARKLY

She shook her head. "No, shut up. I don't want to hear it. You know what I'm talking about. We're done." She waved an arm towards Firl. "There's nothing here. We were just the unfortunate subjects of a last-shot experiment, and now we're going home. That's all."

"No." Mai rushed over, turned her to face her with a crude grab at her arm. "You don't get to do that. You can't tell me this will change nothing for you. That when you go home, you'll take nothing with you. Look at this place! The last hope of a whole universe, and you made your way in here!"

"And for what?" Noll pulled her arm away. She took a shambling step away from everyone, even Jayce, and especially Firl. She was shaking, fear and frustration pummelling her chest. "The only thing I'm taking with me is dread. And that's nothing new. We almost died in this ruined, hopeless universe, what else am I supposed to do with this?"

She turned away, the sudden urge to hit something scaring even her. The sound of awkward shuffling came from the direction of the Nefirns, and Noll suddenly felt self-conscious. It wasn't like her to yell out her hopelessness to a room full of unfortunate souls. Gods damnit. She planted her hands on her waist, not looking at anyone, trying to regulate her breathing.

"Can we go? Let's just go," she muttered. Back to Duplex. Back to her life where she at least knew what to watch out for. None of this multiverse, self-defining, existential crap.

A touch on her shoulder. Somehow, she knew exactly who it was. Her mind leafed through the memories of the hours she'd spent cooped up on the *Taro* with Noll-2, and she was pretty sure this was the first time they actually touched. She had the strange expectation that something should have collapsed or maybe exploded, as a consequence, but there was nothing, only her doppelganger's cool fingers on her skin.

"I'm terrified, too," Noll-2 said quietly. "Please, don't leave like this."

Noll turned back to her, a reaction to some strange magnetism she couldn't deny. Her own face stared into hers from up close. And she knew that look—she felt it in the pull of little muscles in her own cheeks, the ticking of nerves on her forehead, the paralyzed tension of her mouth. Gunshots on a rain- and neon-drenched road, staring at the door praying the boots on the other side wouldn't kick it in the next moment. Huddling in a run-down bar while mutters about a world-killing machine ebbed and flowed around her, anxiety thumping—*should we leave? Is this serious? What does it all mean?*—its jittery song along her whole body.

Her parents disappearing in the open gates of the spaceport, the bitter taste of disappointment slipping over her dry tongue and down her throat to make a nest of distrust in her core. She dealt by not thinking about it. But how could she when it was staring her in the face?

"You're right. We're nothing. Small and weak. How could we ever change anything?" Noll-2 said. "But riddle me this: can we afford not to try? We have to, for the ones we can't live without. We try because otherwise the people we love might be lost." She inclined her head towards the two Jayces, and Liepok, and Mai. "We're small, and we're nothing, and even then, sometimes, we take our rickety ship and jump into a dangerous space-time tunnel leading into the unknown to save our brother."

Temak gave an entertained huff. "Oh, yeah. Or we follow some bad ideas from a stranger we've got no reason to listen to, because it's better than doing nothing."

"Even worse! We follow a person we love, even though we think they're wrong." Mai stepped up to Noll-2 with a faint smile on her lips.

"And we trust, even though everything tells us it's dangerous." That was Liepok. They too were, astonishingly, smiling.

THROUGH A WINDOW DARKLY

Noll's chest ached, the emotion roiling in her stomach. She hated this. She hated it so much. She glanced at Jayce, and to her surprise, her brother was nodding along, a determined look on his face.

She could do nothing but shake her head. This was the worst.

"I know this is a lot," her double said. She glanced at Mai, then back to her. "There are, apparently, many parallel universes, and some of them are just as miserable as ours is. So, what? Mai thinks this limits us or whatever, but do you really think there are 'good' or 'bad' universes? Nah. There are no easy paths. We gotta carve our bloody way out every single time, otherwise we're lost."

That felt true. That, at least, felt right. And hearing it from her own mouth...was something.

"That's the only sense or plan there is, I think," Noll-2 went on. "We fight against unbelievable odds because gods damn, what else can we do? What if no one else is gonna save our brother? What if no one else tries to put things right? We might not succeed, but what the hells. That's why Firl is right. The waves we make can matter. If nothing else, than to those who matter to us."

Noll sighed. "What do you want me to say? I understand, but none of it changes this...this thing." She clawed at her throat, desperate to show where the fear was choking the life out of her, every day, every single day. Did the others see it? Could they feel it? Would that make *her* feel better?

Jayce caught her hand gently. "I'm here. We're with you."

"How is this so easy for you?" It came out as a sob, but she didn't care anymore.

Her brother's smile turned into a slight frown. "Because you're with me, stupid. How else?"

And just like that, things weren't as bad anymore. They were, yes, but also not. Two things could be true at the same time.

He was here with her. If she didn't come through...would Firl have ended up sending him back? Would they have ever seen each other again? Maybe.

Maybe not.

She could be deadly afraid and brave at the same time.

"I just want you to not give up. Not yet." Noll-2 said quietly.

A shiver wafted through Noll, but this time, it was strangely calming. She felt the agents' eyes on her. It was too late for this world. For their two universes, not yet.

Could knowledge change it all? Knowing about this destruction; about how Noll could have had another life where she returned from brainwashing. Where, though drowning in fear, she searched for a better future. Where she still kept the same people in her heart and corrected the path of someone else.

"And anyway. Don't underestimate luck, either." Noll-2 gave an easy shrug. "Sometimes, we come together in certain ways. We may happen upon some...things we can use to stick it to those all-powerful forces high above us, instead of just surviving."

Noll pulled an eyebrow up, but her double was already whirling around towards Firl. "You said you can take us home? You're coming, right?"

The Talalan who had been quietly observing the exchange, reared back, surprised. "Well, I...I never planned— I didn't think— You see, I'm not sure I can make the journey. All that radiation...I'm too weakened. I honestly thought I would die here."

Whatever confidence had been in them before vanished now. They looked small, uncertain. Lonely.

To be alone when everything went dark. Noll had gone mad thinking about Jayce leaving her. What Firl must be feeling was unimaginable.

"Would you try?" Noll asked. She cleared her throat; her voice was hoarse. "This doesn't have to be the end for you. You've done a lot."

THROUGH A WINDOW DARKLY

Firl smiled warily. "You've forgiven me?"

Noll sighed. She was so tired. But the question was, she had to admit, absurd. "If everything's like you said it is, there's nothing to forgive. You were just trying...trying to do something."

"Like us," Jayce added. Noll narrowed her eyes at him—at all the others, standing there, smiling like they understood some solution to a puzzle she couldn't even see. But she couldn't help it—the tension in her chest released as she looked over the group, all alive, all safe now. They'd done this.

Home. They were going home after all. With this impossible knowledge forever accompanying them. She looked at the others, this ridiculous, motley crew of friends and strangers. They would only have to decide what to do with what they'd learned.

Well, alright, she thought as Firl started awkwardly explaining to Noll-2 and Jayce-2 about their last operational shuttle which they could take to get out of this collapsing universe, and Mai squinted at her with an all-knowing, gentle expression on her face, and Temak clapped a hand on Liepok's shoulder and made some easy comment to Captain Frahyss and the Krotke twins (times two) that made them all grin.

Noll held onto Jayce's hand even tighter, and her twin squeezed back. *Alright. Everything is still fucked up, y'all won't convince me it's not. But this...this ought to be interesting, maybe.*

8

Noll Morgan sat in the main room of The Candle with a drink in her hand. The space was empty, apart from three locals engaged in a heated conversation at a table next to the door and Saori quietly talking to her assistant, Bernard, behind the counter. It was after breakfast but too early for the lunch crowd. She took a long gulp from the drink, some feisty purple-colored liqueor she'd already forgotten the name of. Her eyes lingered on the door, and she sighed when nothing happened.

It had only been a day, but it felt like several centuries. Saying goodbye to their parallel-universe doubles and frenemies, taking the *Taro* through the Window back to Duplex, watching the gateway flicker once, twice, then return to its nominal state for good...dodging and surviving all the questions from county patrol, lane scientists, and lanehunter clan big wigs, and finally crashing in their respective beds—it all seemed like a fever dream. Noll was surprised they apparently all kept their stories straight in the chaos, but they must have, since there was a distinct lack of a suspicious-slash-intrigued crowd gathering in front of the restaurant (or around Liepok's giant spaceship) this morning, demanding they further explain the Window's loony anomalies.

"We don't know what happened. We crossed over, fished the people who got pulled through out of the vacuum of space, waited around in desperation for a couple of hours, and then when we saw Duplex through the Window again, we came back."

It helped that the gateway was back to normal now. Locals wanted things to calm down, and a lot of the outworlders didn't have much context to what had happened. The Krotke twins had taken most of the heat, also, known and popular as they were around here, and since they acted all convincing and chill about things, people tended to go with it.

And Noll made sure the twins had a good reason to act convincing and chill.

"Hey, stupid!" Jayce's sharp voice cut through the ennui. He clattered down the stairs and through the open door leading up to The Candle's first floor, eyes half open, hair disheveled. He'd decided to spend the night in one of Saori's guest rooms instead of his bunk on the *Taro* for the sake of better sleep—no matter how much he tried to power through, he felt weak and drained after his short adventure in the cold void and low pressure of outer space. Now as he weaved towards Noll among the tables and plopped onto the seat across from her, he seemed healthier but still exhausted. "You're up early."

"And you're up late." Noll dipped her glass towards her brother in greeting. "How are you feeling?"

Jayce rolled his shoulders. "Like my body nearly froze over while the blood boiled in my veins and all the oxygen got sucked out of my lungs." He sighed wistfully. Then he winked and leaned back on the chair. Noll rolled her eyes, but her throat constricted painfully at the thought of it.

"Too soon," She met his glance, and Jayce seemed to sober up. She didn't let him apologize. "You gotta eat something," she added, already stretching her neck to catch Saori's gaze.

"Yes, momma," Jayce sulked but didn't argue. He'd just have to make peace with Noll being more protective and mothering than usual. Since she generally wasn't like that at all, it was a hard adjustment. For both of them. "So, when's your date? Soon, huh?"

Noll glared at him. "It's not a date. We're all meeting Temak for lunch in the Silver Beaver. I think we said twelve o'clock?"

Jayce smirked. "But maybe you wanna go alone? To this not-date?"

"No." Noll grunted in frustration. Against all her efforts, heat still sprung in her cheeks. The point of the meeting (not date!) was for their wayward little group to catch up again after the whirlwind of yesterday—they had a lot to talk about. She couldn't entertain the thought of...whatever Jayce was insinuating. Not yet. "We can go soon, but I'm waiting for someone."

As if on cue, the door to The Candle swung in and a grinning Liepok marched through it. Saori, who was already circling the bar and heading towards the twins, stopped and watched them approach.

The Nefirn actually had a spring in their step. Noll had never seen them this cheerful before.

"Good morning," Liepok greeted all three of them with nods, one after the other. The locals near the door stopped arguing, sizing the newcomer up with suspicion. A sociable Nefirn? Here? Scandalous.

"Morning, morning," Jayce replied. He stood and clapped their shoulder gently. "What's new?" He'd been quick to warm up to the Nefirn, especially after finding out they'd saved Noll's life.

Liepok smiled at Jayce. "Are you feeling better?"

"Much better. How about your friends?"

The smile got a shade less intense. "Fine. I think, for now, they want to forget about what happened. They won't." They turned to Noll and hurried to add, "But they will not tell. They understand it can be dangerous."

"Yeah, well." Noll waved a hand around, lowering her voice. "Make sure they know whatever they decide, we'll need to do it together."

Liepok nodded. That was when Saori reached them, and the silence that enveloped the group as the innkeeper stopped by them was, unfortunately, telling.

Saori planted her hands on her waist with a frown. "Good morning to all of you."

They all muttered the same back to her. The innkeeper was, understandably suspicious of them, especially after they'd gotten her uncle Wal out of his high-tech hidey-hole and into the *Taro* for a half an hour last night, after which the old man had turned just as secretive and cagey as the group about all the things Saori didn't yet know.

But they had to keep the details secret for now. At least until they thought through all the implications and angles. It was honestly a bit scary.

Noll rolled her eyes again. So much fuss about something she wasn't even sure was happening. But the nagging feeling at the back of her mind had not relented since they'd left Firl's research station behind.

It was like her doppelganger had said. Sometimes, even though you felt useless and tiny in the grand scheme of things, you happened upon something special that could be used to change things. To ignore it would have been very dumb.

"Don't squander this away," her other self told her in the shadowy dock area before her group got onto the Talalan shuttle. "I'll come through and beat you up, I swear."

Noll pulled up an eyebrow. "Physical threats, eh? I usually do those when I'm intimidated. Good to know where we stand."

Noll-2 just gave her a crooked smile. "Oh, we're not that similar, you and I."

Mai sidled up beside them, shaking her head. "Do we have a problem here? Even after all this?"

The two Nolls stared at each other and relented with a faint smile at the same time. "Nah," Noll said. She felt spectacularly awkward, and this pretend-beef wasn't helping as much as she'd hoped. This was, more than likely, the last time they all saw each other, and she wasn't sure how she was supposed to file that away.

She still reared back when Noll-2 went in for a hug. It was a long one, too.

"Take care, okay?" her doppelganger muttered into her ear. "Watch out for your brother. Don't be stupid." She drew back and held her away to look her in the eyes. "And if you manage to...get up to some shenanigans, do let us know somehow."

THROUGH A WINDOW DARKLY

Noll nodded. All of it felt unreal. "What are you gonna do, though? Are you sure you don't want Firl to go with you?"

"No, you need them more," Mai had said, throwing a look at Noll-2. "We still have connections with the Union, and now that we know what we're looking for, I think we can come up with something fun by ourselves."

Noll jarred herself out of the memory. Saori was talking.

"—and I don't know what you're planning with Wallace, but I don't like it. You're not telling me something." She fixed a strict look at Noll. "And you should. I can help."

Noll gave her a faint smile. Her fingers found that tear in her jacket and picked at it, a nervous habit she'd taken up the last day or so. "No one said you cannot come to the Beaver at twelve o'clock to hear us out." She shrugged. "But a warning: whatever you'll hear, you can't unhear it. You'll have to be sure you want it."

It was risky to involve Saori, especially after the things she'd recently gone through involving all kinds of other lane-related madness. But Noll also had to admit, they could use her. If nothing else, she'd tell her fair and square if this idea of hers was total bullshit. And maybe...maybe she needed that.

"Let's go, then," Saori said forcefully, glancing at the clock on the wall. It was a bit early, but Noll wouldn't have been surprised if Temak was already there, waiting for them. When she'd shared her musings with him before they'd said goodbye the previous night, he was...well, electrified would have been an understatement.

Before Noll could have answered, the door opened again, and Mai walked in. This universe's Mai. The one that didn't know her yet.

Noll followed her with her glance subtly as the ex-agent made her way to one of the tables in the back and sat, melting into the background. She was good at that.

Saori was waiting for her answer, so she said, standing, "You can go ahead. I'll follow in a sec."

Jayce looked at Mai, then back to her. He got the message. "Oh...oh yeah. Actually, yes. Let's go, everyone. We'll talk about enigmatic things and vague plans and uh, conspiracies or whatever. This is gonna be fun."

It wasn't like Noll had made a promise or anything. But it was something she had to try.

Jayce shepherded the confused Saori and Liepok towards the door. Liepok's smile returned; they were excited to be involved, and although that could change when they understood what they were in for, Noll knew she could expect a calm and kind viewpoint from the Nefirn whenever the opinions needed to collide. That was good, having many sides, especially if the Krotkes kept blackmailing themselves into the middle of Noll's plans, too.

Saori's expression, in contrast, turned even more clouded as she listened to Jayce's blabbering, but her curiosity must have proven stronger, and the three of them walked out into the sunny morning, leaving Noll temporarily alone.

Her brother threw her a knowing look from the threshold, and Noll saluted him with a grin. *Nice one, stupid.*

Everything was easier together.

She turned towards Mai, only a bit uncertain. She made her posture relaxed and casual as she walked up to her table, even though her heart kept bonking into her ribs in a chaotic rhythm. Mai had been lurking around last evening when the group was making their rounds with the locals and the clan goons explaining themselves and lying through their teeth, but she never got too close and never said a word to them.

Now, as Noll approached her, the woman raised her head, a confused look flashing through her face.

"Hey," Noll started. She scratched at the tear in her jacket again, hooking a finger through the small hole. "Mai, right? I'm Noll. Noll Morgan."

A small frown appeared on the other's face. "I know who you are."

THROUGH A WINDOW DARKLY

She'd offered Noll her help, back in No Man's Land, and Noll ignored it. It had been probably for the best, at that time. But things were different now.

Hard boots against concrete on rain-drenched streets. Explosions in the distance; destroyers hovering in the sky. Lanes swallowing up an entire universe, people, untrusting, terrified, running towards their bitter end. Things had to change. Noll had to allow them to change.

"No, you don't," she said. "That's none of your fault, though. Can I sit and talk to you for a moment? I think I need you for something...brave."

Mai's frown deepened. The tear in Noll's jacket ripped further as she accidentally yanked at it, and she pulled her finger out, trying to smooth the textile over, pretend her fiddling could mend the hole.

Suddenly, the analogy hit her, and she had to grin. She thought about her brother sitting down with Temak and the others in the Beaver, a conspiring look on his face. She thought about Firl, hiding on the *Taro* with the plans for their multiverse-opening all-powerful lane-manipulator, waiting for them anxiously. She thought about the lane-crisscrossed hellscape of the Talalan's doomed universe: innumerable tears on the expansive fabric of space-time.

And two huge fingers, pinching the material together to sew it back again.

No, it was not the solution. It might not even help. But it was a start to take things into their hands.

Mai's face was still as a statue as she spoke. "I don't know what you want from me. I'm useful, sometimes. But not brave, so."

Noll nodded. "I know. That's okay." She sat and winked at her, enjoying Mai's absolutely uncomprehending look before going on. "Me neither. Wanna do something weird together, still?"

Acknowledgements

I'm thankful to the writer community of the HuNo Discord and the enjoyers of its Choose Your Own Adventure channel who were willing to immerse themselves in my world and directed my hand in assembling this story.

HELYNA L. CLOVE

If you enjoyed these adventures, check out *Skylark in the Fog*, taking place in the same universe, featuring even more flying around in space, weird wormhole troubles, and a found family to write home about! And if you have a moment to spare, consider giving a review or star on whatever platform you prefer. It all helps getting the word out about these stories, and will make the author (me) really happy!

You can also find out more about me and my books by visiting helynalclove.com, and if you'd like to stay up-to-date with my work, join my monthly newsletter Transmissions from The Clove Cove there!

About the Author

Helyna L. Clove (she/they) is a science-fiction/fantasy novelist, and a lover of all types of storytelling, hot comfort drinks, and a universe full of stars.

She was born in Hungary and raised in a small village a few miles off the shores of Lake Balaton. She was often described by her teachers as someone always having "her head in the clouds", and she spent the first fifteen years of her life mostly consuming books from her parents' home library, watching some great 90's sci-fi shows, and working on her eclectic music taste. After several arduous years of obtaining her astrophysics degree, she currently lives in Wales with her small family of a wonderful boyfriend and Puddle, the tortoiseshell cat. Her debut novel was *Skylark in the Fog*, an epic space opera published in 2022.

When not writing her stories, she can be found commandeering radio telescopes, reading, cooking, playing video games, or trying her hand at different art forms.

www.ingramcontent.com/pod-product-compliance
Ingram Content Group UK Ltd.
Pitfield, Milton Keynes, MK11 3LW, UK
UKHW022240210325
456590UK00005BA/53